THE CARD READER

By Bill Morris

☽ ☾ ☆
New ☽ Sun Publications

Half Moon Bay, California

For information contact:

newsunpub@aol.com

New Sun Publications

227 Granelli Ave
Half Moon Bay, Ca 94019

To the Fools everywhere, you know who you are.

~Bill

READINGS

CHAPTER 1

"Welcome," I said, "sit down here at my table. The cards are friendly today. Let's learn what we learn."

CHAPTER 2

She was fifteen and smiling. She had long blond hair that hung at the sides of her head in strings, except that one strand had a fluffy magenta feather tied to it, like the left-over remnant of a good dream stuck in mussed hair. Her arms were slender, she was underdeveloped, but she tilted her head with charm and a tea-saucer smile. One wrist dangled a brass ID bracelet, her other hand covered with small rings of glittering metals.

She was a young girl trying hard.

When she spoke, she used the diction of a young woman, but chattering laughter was not far behind.

She still wore jeans and tennis shoes without socks.

"Good morning," she said first.

"Morning," I said. "Would you like to know something?" She was standing hesitant in the doorway, hand on doorknob, heel down, toe up.

"Ah huh," she said, nodding.

"Is it something about feathers?" I asked, "I notice you have one lodged in your hair."

She laughed. "Well, maybe."

"I don't know if I should come in and see you."

"Sorry, too late, I've lost the power to become invisible on command." I shrugged raising my hands briefly from the table.

"Once you've seen me here, I'm stuck."

"Does it cost much?" she asked.

Newcomer questions. The people who know me never ask.

"The cost is usually acceptable, because you decide what you'll pay."

"Even if I don't have much?" She looked at me with lifted brow.

"I accept IOU's payable in the next generation," I said.

She had to think about that for a second.

"You mean you'd take my first baby or something?"

I laughed. "No, I mean that you don't have to pay me if you don't want to, and what you take you will owe to the next generation after you. You must pass it on to them."

"I don't get it," she said. She was charming and young in her bewilderment. Her two hands had dove into her pockets for an instant and then come out again. I could tell she really wanted to see me.

"Sit down," I said.

She came forward and sat with her hands in her lap like a good school girl.

I took out my cards wrapped luxuriously in a black silk scarf with rainbow edge. I unfolded the scarf to expose the deck as if I were unwrapping a sandwich.

"And your question is?" I asked. I smiled. I raised an eyebrow. I tilted my head in encouragement. I tried not to look like an old crow looking at a crumb. But she was funny and I liked her.

"I want to know about the future," she said. She pressed her lips to seal them in an uneasy half-smile.

"It's all in front of you," I said. I looked at her until she got it and laughed.

"What's wrong with you?" she laughed.

I shrugged. "I'm a gypsy card reader."

That's always explanation enough.

I threw a few cards. I told her of the wonderful things inside her. I made her leave without paying.

"Go on now, don't worry about money," I said.

She smiled and made just the smallest hand wave. And after she shut the door, she made one skip as she walked away.

I hoped she would stay forever young.

Seeing some people is a gift in itself.

CHAPTER 3

I threw this card for her: The Fool.

"It is a time of new beginnings. You must be the happy fool."

She looked at me in her stiff white collar and blue suit coat. She was a well known fashion designer, but her business was toppling.

"No way, I'm an expert!"

"You must throw all that away, you must start over."

She looked at me without blinking.

"Just take it under advisement. You're beginning a new path, a new journey. Be happy. Be confident. Open to it."

She sat back. I could see her vision of herself budge.

"Maybe," she said, then half to herself, "Right now I couldn't even sell a pair of socks."

I looked at her until we both laughed.

It was her first step on a new path. It requires a happy blind faith.

CHAPTER 4

I'm not much interested in stories, including my own. I'm a card reader. I deal with the internal truth and the eternal. My cards don't tell stories. They tell the truth.

Most people are interested in their stories, the possessions grabbed, money won squeezed lost, lovers mounted, competitors bested, speakable and unspeakable acts. I'm not so interested. Most are just telling stories to themselves without knowing the ending.

They come to me when they get stuck.

So I throw my tarot cards on the table.

I give them a reading. I see the grimaces, sighs, blustery angers, regurgitated sobs, yodels of regret, laughs of recognition, snickers of mischief. I've even had a woman vomit with self-disgust.

And, of course, I see the beatific, well-formed gods and goddesses, young as ever, full of life, sexual vitality, waiting for the next great page of their stories to be read.

I read and say what the cards teach. I tell them things about themselves they have forgotten.

Things they must remember to live.

And then they can start telling their stories again.

CHAPTER 5

"These cards are true," he said.

He was hunched and thick-necked looking at the cards. He had a squat round head, black hair, but balding. Chest hair showed from the neck of his flannel shirt.

He was frowning, a sour Buddha, his mouth working like a mole munching through dirt.

I had turned three reversed cards of earth. There was turmoil in his home.

"My wife is cheating on me," he said. He spoke it to the cards, then rubbed his chin. His voice was husky with anger.

"We've been married 14 years. Our two kids are twelve and thirteen. Now she goes and does this. They'll live in poverty, this happens."

I nodded.

"Christ," he said, pushing at the cards.

"Why'd she do this? My fucking sister's husband."

I turned over the final card of the throw.

It was the Earth Father, reversed. A card of great fertility and power, bringing forth from the earth. But it was reversed.

"More disruption," I said.

He sat stone silent. Then he clenched his thick hands.

He got up and went to the door without paying. I realized he would slam it behind him.

"Don't kill your wife," I said.

His back stiffened as if I'd shot an arrow. Then the door cracked like a pistol.

I only read the cards. I seldom deny them.

CHAPTER 6

I saw something unearthly in her. She was tall, pale and drawn. But her face was refined and angelic. She walked in wearing a black coat, black shirt, black pants. She was utterly silent as her eyes swept once around the reading room.

I sat watching her without a word.

Then she was sitting before me. I didn't know how she'd moved there or sat.

She looked down at the table and nodded.

Her face had the beautiful chiselled features of a cat. She sat, staring at my table.

I began turning over cards.

"What do you want to know?" I asked.

She looked at me. There was immense knowing in her eyes. She shook her head. She didn't need to answer.

I read the throw.

All wind cards. Powerful wind. Beautiful wind, and the reversed Prince of Wind.

"You know something," I said. "Beyond what is normal."

She sat motionless.

She put out a hand to the edge of the table. Shaking.

Her beautiful face had not changed. She sat looking at the cards.

"You know something. Something beyond the realms of this earth," I said.

Her eyes rose from the table. I felt a tremendous thrill as she looked at me.

"What do you know?" I asked.

She got up and went to the door. She did not look back or say anything as she left the door open.

"What do you know!" I called out after her into the darkness. Car lights were already spinning past her like shooting stars.

She never looked back.

CHAPTER 7

"My son is uncontrollable." Her son was thirteen. He was screaming, pushing her around. Drinking. Swearing. In trouble at school. Now arrested.

Her face was too thin and constrained. She blinked like an owl.

I knew he was lost.

I threw four cards. Dirty water and dirty wind.

"Your son is a reflection of yourself, a reflection of your needs. You have no answers."

"I've tried to tell him how to live right," she gripped her small purse in her lap, elbows out. Indignant.

My gypsy blood makes me see these people as peasants.

"How do I change him? I'm afraid of him. He's stealing my money. He's always angry. He never comes home. Now arrested for fighting."

"He hasn't given up yet."

"Why can't he give up and just be a good boy?" Her brow furrowed as if she were thinking. "How do I change him?"

I knew she drank. Screamed. A real mother.

I turned over an earth card.

"You can't change him. You have no answers. You must change."

I turned over The Sun.

"You must turn to the sun. You must grow."

Now she was on her feet. Her face was expanding. Her eyebrows were daggers.

"I've worked hard to teach that damn boy!" Then she had nothing to say. She was searching for the moral high ground.

She stomped out without leaving a penny.

On The Sun are three sunflowers. One facing the sun, but most facing away.

CHAPTER 8

People think I live in the little room behind the shop. I don't, I actually have an apartment across town. It's an older building with no concierge, but the elevator has a chrome door. Trees and flowering birds of paradise in the lobby. Large glass windows everywhere, the hallmarks of modern life.

I live on a large trust that my ancestors generously put aside for me. My father owned the building and the apartment is permanently deeded to me. I pay little attention to the investments and annuities set up. Just letting the abundance of the earth ride, so to speak.

I drove an ochre jaguar when I was in my twenties.

But it makes no sense as a card reader, so I gave it up. I take buses across town. My pockets always seem filled with change anyway. I like seeing people.

Funny, a stockbroker comes into my shop, I know exactly what he's worried about. I could tell him which commodities to put a put on. But I'm not here to offer gambling advice.

The few who've learned the truth, that I eat paté as I listen to Jacque Borrell and French pop music on the stereo, a Gauguin and a Monet (restored) on the wall, a daily bouquet from the florist my one vice, they wonder why I have my little shop at all.

But really, there's no question. Not if you understand the power of the cards inside you. I choose it as a way of life.

Gypsies. You know how they are.

CHAPTER 9

Slender, elegant, and tentative, she looked at me with a half smile. A recent divorce. She had blond hair that was so clean it flowed like water. She smiled and talked from a tilted head. As I shuffled she leaned in.

I could imagine her light breath falling on the cards.

"I want to know if I should do something," she said. She swallowed with worry.

I nodded. She smiled and shrugged.

"Let's begin," I said, regally.

"Have you ever had a tarot reading before?"

She smirked and grimaced and shook her head.

"Good," I said. "Close your eyes and think of your greatest fear."

She looked at me with small lines under her eyes. Then she closed them and thought. Her forehead frowned.

"Now, open your eyes and look at me. Think of your greatest desire."

She looked at me. I looked back half-smiling in welcome.

I drew a single card from the deck. It was The Fool.

"This is a tarot card," I said holding it up like a thin blade toward her. "It's a very thin card. It has two sides. On one side is the image, the other side blocks the view."

I showed both sides of the card.

"They are two sides of the same card. And here is the secret. If you can see, resolve or achieve what is on one side, you see, resolve or achieve what is on the other."

She was looking at me listening hard.

I smiled. "It is a friendly card. It is inside you."

Her face became utterly beautiful and open.

I slipped the card back in the deck and set the deck beside me.

"That's it?" she laughed. "A one card reading? What about my question?"

"You should do it."

She laughed and made the gesture of kissing the back of her hand.

She put her head back and laughed again.

"How much do I owe you?"

"Nothing."

"Nothing?"

"I'm independently wealthy." I inclined my head.

"I owe you something."

"You owe me your old life," I smiled. "I have already taken it. Now you must start a new life for yourself."

She laughed and rose from the chair. She was happy. Incredulous.

"I could kiss you," she said.

“There’s no stopping you,” I said.

And then she did.

I felt independently wealthy.

CHAPTER 10

She had the turned-up nose and why-not expression of a Pekinese. She wore a fur collar and a bird nest hat with small flowers peeking out. Her cat was Persian, fat and smug.

She wanted a reading for her pet.

“Why don’t you do readings for animals?” Her forehead blistering with dissatisfaction.

“There’s not much animal there,” I said. I gestured a knuckle toward the smug lump.

She didn’t like that. She wanted the cat’s future read.

I thought about pulling the Death card from the pack and just laying it on him.

I shook my head. I opened my hands as if to catch the bird nest if it fell.

She had an expensive purse as big as her cat. She hoisted both under each arm as she left.

It was a fantastic show of cowardice.

A woman trying to live through her cat.

CHAPTER 11

Each time she came to see me her silk shirt was unbuttoned one more button. This was the fourth reading. I could see the goblet-curve of a breast.

She was calm, waiting, with a falcon's pride in her nose and mouth.

I could imagine opening her blouse like curtains on the theatre of her sexuality.

I reached out and put both hands in her blouse. I spread it.

She looked at me proudly and said, "Yes."

CHAPTER 12

As a card reader I'm nearly invisible. Clients only see me as a first impression, before I start reading cards. They see a dark-haired man, handsome in face graced with focused brow and eyes, a gypsy mustache, a pleasing smile with fine white teeth. I wear a work costume to match people's expectations, a red shirt and a black vest flowery with gold brocade. I wear black jeans with black boots hidden under the cuffs. Within a boot sleeps a knife I keep for crazy or murderous ones. I have an occasional attempted robbery.

I laugh at them, what are they going to take? My deck?

That usually pisses the crazy, the murderous, the robbers off.

I pull my knife and we come to terms.

"One step further and you'll read your future in your own entrails," I once said.

I'm sure Clint Eastwood would have loved that.

But mainly, I sit calmly before my clients. Unremarkable. No scars, no ear ring, no black eye patch. No leer at the women, no facade of comforting disinterest for the men. I remain casual and comfortable so my client can be.

My reading room is decorated with just enough articles, family pictures, a stuffed chair with arm doilies, end tables draped with colored cloth and knickknacks, shaded yellow lamps, so that the room, like me, is complete and not overbearing.

My table, like a great black lily pad, sits waiting in the center of the room. Clients on entering feel they must immediately come in and sit at it. Then they take a second glance at me, and another about the room. Then the reading is ready to begin.

After I turn over the first card and explain, I become invisible. I know it immediately. The man or woman freezes, listening intensely, staring down at the card now a spotlight. You'd think they'd been hypnotized and told they couldn't raise their eyes. As I turn card after card, it makes no difference how I look, the cards are all that can be seen.

CHAPTER 13

She put down her brief case. It was chrome and leather. Her hair was cut short with one feminine wing on her forehead. Her pretty face was closed and her mouth straight, her clothes a dark blue jacket, straight skirt, and loafers. There was no sense of sexuality about her. She sat and looked at me evenly.

"I want to know if I should quit my job," she said.

"Why?" I asked.

She shrugged. "It's so..." Her mouth opened and she inhaled and swallowed bitterly.

It was tearing her up inside.

I turned several cards, placing them face down, reading the laundry list aloud.

"In your job I see jealousy, social climbing, anger, rude behavior, unresolved family issues being worked out inappropriately. I see lack of vision, placeholding, uncaring, contaminating bitterness, fear, insecurity, betrayal, money grubbing."

"That's the job all right." To her credit she smiled.

"You must work for a bank," I said.

That made her laugh. I felt I'd succeeded.

"No, my job is in mid-town corporate America," she said.

I turned over a card. I didn't need to look.

"It is spiritually bankrupt," I said.

“Most people would say it is incredibly successful. Our beloved corporate America.”

“It isn’t in the cards,” I said. I turned over the next card without looking down at it.

“Why?”

“Corporations are great at producing goods and services and amassing vast sums of capital. But those vast sums have no spiritual goal, are not directed toward a larger humanitarian end. Our goods and services are only for the few who can afford them.”

“We are the success of the world,” she said with a disbelieving sigh.

“A wise man once said something. It was that your biggest strength is also you greatest weakness.”

“Who was that? Confucius?” Her nose wrinkled with amusement.

“No, his name was Randy, a software marketing guy.”

She raised her throat and laughed like a bird drinking.

“I just want to know about my job,” she said pleasantly.

I turned over the next card.

“There’s something missing,” I said.

She raised her shoulders and tilted her head in a question.

“It’s you,” I said.

CHAPTER 14

The Tower.

He was a college student and he sat solemn faced. He'd learned something. He sat apprehensive and worried before me.

"I don't really believe in this stuff," he said, squeezing his hands in his lap.

"Sure you do," I said.

"What did you learn? Something has shaken you. When you pull The Tower, it is a feeling of the world tumbling down. A sense of division. The foundations don't hold. It's a very unsettling time. You are upset. The calm tower of protection you have erected is falling."

"Yes," he said.

I turned the Wind Father.

"Is it about God?" I asked.

He only swallowed in answer. He hoisted his shoulders like a heavy yoke.

"You have learned that God has your Father's face," I said.

"There is no freedom. No real happiness, just struggle."

I turned over the Five of Wind. Fear.

"Your fears are holding you back. It is a time of worry, and a sense of futility. See the swords? They are broken at the tips. You feel you have no alternatives. The swords are making a wall blocking you."

"How do you change the face of God?" he asked, half of his face pulled sideways with pain.

"You must choose new beliefs," I said.

"Choose new beliefs. How? If it's true, it's true."

I shook my head. "Your beliefs are not in these cards. Nor are they in this table or in that door. They are not outside in the park, nor up in the sky."

He was listening hard to me now. A bit hunched, but listening.

"They are sitting in that chair," I said.

I picked up all the cards mixing them, then spread them across the entire table like a great weaving serpent.

"Here is a lesson of the Tarot," I said.

"After The Tower come these three cards," I said.

I placed The Sun, The Moon, and The Star, before him.

"These are just ahead of you," I said.

"They are wonderful cards."

CHAPTER 15

There are certain cards that always appear like gems to me. They lie on the black tablecloth shining. Shining so it's hard for me to reach out and turn them over.

Two of Earth: cause and effect (it has a gleaming rainbow twisting into infinity like a bow tie).

The Water Mother (sitting calm in Lotus position, resolute, and loving).

The Fool.

The Star

The Moon.

The Sun.

I suppose it's because I still want to live. And so of all the cards, I cherish these cards of empowerment.

My first Tarot teacher told me, "Never weep before the cards."

I asked why.

"Because, it does little good, it doesn't change things. It doesn't change the cards."

She shrugged, "Besides, it makes them sticky for the next shuffle."

CHAPTER 16

"Do you believe in the cards?" she challenged. "Really?"

She was thirty-three and a bit drawn in the face.

"The important thing is if you hear something that you think is true, will you believe it?" I asked.

Then I gave her a reading of 23 cards, and told her exactly what I thought was true until she was ready to fall in love with me.

CHAPTER 17

He danced in the ballet.

He always came alone. He was not effeminate. He'd just chosen art and it had isolated him. Although women threw themselves at him, it was because they were isolated from their feminine sides, and they meant nothing to him. Communicating through his body on stage was all he had, and it was not enough. His art appealed to the few, if at all. The general populace on hearing he danced was encouraging, standoffish, then had nothing to say.

He spent hours alone practicing in a loft. He sweated and groaned and twisted in pain and loneliness.

He said, "Like a fish in an aquarium, I know how to live there."

He wanted to know when he would die.

I always pulled the Wind Sister. The card of the triumph of knowing, of poetry, and of the beautiful escaping butterflies of art.

He would nod and leave. Solemn.

A prisoner returning to his special cell.

Somewhere I knew pictures of him hung in the empty halls of the theatre. The hallways he walked between moments of bright lights and beauty.

CHAPTER 18

The history of the cards is a long one. They are a codification of an ancient esoteric branch of Hebraic knowledge, the Kaballa. A secret knowledge only given men over forty after they'd attained a certain education and wisdom. Personally, I think every teenager in America should be schooled in the fundamentals of the cards, so maybe they'd have some means of understanding their internal worlds as opposed to working through youthful dilemmas blind, suffering the pain of trial¬-and-error. Knowing the Tree of Life could help.

I mainly see the cards as a body of primitive psychology. A map of human internals, feelings, and fundamentals that the ancients remarked. And it's all very unscientific. But just because the ancients didn't run a hamster through a maze to prove humans have a heart, a spirit, a mind, a will, a clumsy selfish beautifully willing body, that doesn't mean these fundamentals aren't worth knowing.

I've read the history of the cards, dominated by mystic scholars from the medieval Philippus Aureolus Theophrastus Bombastus von Hohenheim (Paracelus for short), Court de Gébelin, Alphonse Louis Constant, A.E. Waite and the boys of the Golden Dawn, to Paul Foster Case and the Builders of the Adytum, Dion Fortune, Gareth Knight, Aleister Crowley and so on. And coupled with the insights of C. G. Jung, the ringmaster of archetypes, who taught us about symbols and the difference between the internal and external world, and Joseph Cambell's long wonderfully academic and thrilling career of teaching us once again how to read—well, you come to a point where you can read the old ones and the new ones and see what they're getting at.

You realize you too can read the cards.

CHAPTER 19

Strangest requests.

A man asked me if the cards would tell him where the tornado left his dog.

A woman who'd swallowed her wedding ring during sex wanted to know if she should tell her husband who hadn't been there.

An angel-faced policeman wanted to know if the burglar he'd shot but got away had died. (He was hoping yes.)

An insurance agent wanted to know if I could predict car accidents.

A haggard man wanted to know if he should remarry his alcoholic wife a third time. His question: "Was three a charm or was he just stupid?"

"Which vacuum cleaner should I buy?" I recommended the Hoover or the one with the simplest instructions.

"How do you know if you're living or dead?" I told her if you're living people keep sending you bills.

And, of course, "Where did I bury the money?"

CHAPTER 20

Each day is a new vision and new life. A new shuffle so to speak.

Do you want to put on clean clothes or dirty clothes?

The decisions are simple.

CHAPTER 21

"He's cheated. He's lied. He stays out nights, with no excuses. He'll come in shouting, provoking me." She threw back her hair over her shoulder with the gesture of a horse bucking the bridle. Her eyes were blue moons, open and honest.

They had been married barely two years.

"What do you see?" she asked.

She was incredibly handsome. Her shoulders straight, a V-neck descending into a black blouse like a finger pointing to an opal on her chest. Buxom. Grey plaid skirt, tight, held with a patent leather belt.

She put her chin in the goblet of her palm and leaned forward on her elbow to look at me. She was completely at ease.

"Can you tell me what's wrong?" she asked.

I turned over three high cards of earth. Reversed.

"He's afraid of you," I said, "Perhaps because of your sexual prowess."

After a pause, she asked, "Can I change this?"

She straightened in her chair and looked at me levelly.

"No," I said. "He knows he will never be your equal."

CHAPTER 22

When she kissed me, I felt the card of Resurrection. When she held my hand, the Two of Earth. When she whispered in my ear, I felt the pleasure and poetry of the Wind Sister.

When I held her against my chest, I felt the healing of The Lovers.

When I made love to her, I felt the energy charge of the Lightening Path.

In the years I knew her, I moved with her once around the cycle of the Mandala.

It was an immense gift.

With her arms behind her head, she would lie back and cross her legs with my semen still in her, close her eyes, her breasts free and loose, and say,

"Sweetie, do that to me again."

CHAPTER 23

When he walked in, it was death. Top Sergeant, served two tours in Viet Nam. Shot in the leg, retired with a cane and a limp.

He'd tried teaching ROTC at the university but they were boys.

He sat, his eyes black and understanding as gun barrels. His aura told me he could and had killed people in close quarters. I felt uneasy, and intense interest to see what the cards would turn over.

He sat motionless, watching my hands closely.

One of Fire: Force

The troubling Seven of Earth: The Garden

The Mystery Card

Nine of Water: The Rainbow Mirror

The Chariot

The Hierophant

It was going to be a long and difficult reading. I decided to start backwards.

"The Hierophant is calling you to live from your higher self..."

But before I could continue, he reached and pointed to the Mystery Card.

"What does that card mean?" he asked sharply. "I've never seen it in any other decks."

"It is a special card contained only in this deck." I shook my head, "I don't know what it means completely."

He nodded, accepting the honesty of this answer.

"It has something to do with the mystery of life," I said.

He looked at me. He nodded.

"This is a good card," he said. "Where can I get this deck?"

I studied him with realization.

"Do you want me to finish the reading?" I asked.

"No, I've read them."

I handed him my deck. He blinked and was touched.

He put down enough money for the reading and the cards.

"They saved my life once," he said. I nodded and he left.

CHAPTER 24

He was a poet. "I just saw a blackbird smoking a pretzel," he said cheerfully. "Running along with it just like it was a cigarette."

"Strange sightings are yours," I laughed.

Like many, he wrote poems but was hesitant to share them. What made him different I thought was that his poems weren't about himself, they were about what he wanted others to know about themselves.

"I once saw a dog carrying a flashlight like that," I said friendly.

"Search and rescue," he said.

We both laughed.

"Are you writing?" I asked.

He shrugged. It was something he did, it couldn't be helped.

"I saw one of your poems posted on a tree the other day," I said.

"I've decided to skip the middleman and publish right on the uncut forest," he said. "Publishing becomes as easy as a tack."

This was good. I liked this. He had a wonderful way of sweeping away obstacles.

"New things in your life?" I asked.

"Everything," he said.

I didn't understand that, but I laughed and let it pass.

"What's up for today?" I said, lifting my deck in invitation.

"I haven't any money," he said. This was a joke between us. A courtesy.

"Too late, I've already bought the cards," I said. "I have to use them."

"What would you like to know?"

I waited to hear today's question. Would he be asking about gleaming foods made entirely of starlight, rainbows as the final resting place of our tears, the invisible golden bracelets of hope worn by all children? He always had spectacular questions.

I would have paid him to ask.

CHAPTER 25

Very young children are often the hardest to give a reading. They sit before you with all the cards inside them. Yet they haven't seen these cards, it's a new unshuffled deck.

Each card is in the proper order and right-side up.

They just sit there happy, smiling before you, and there isn't much to say.

I usually show them the most beautiful cards just for fun.

They ask me if I drew the pictures.

CHAPTER 26

She had grown up neglected. She'd lived with her mother, mainly reading by herself in her own room. Her mother could become immensely angry. So she had her own world.

Now she was twenty-five, never had a boyfriend, could not brook the idea of touching animals, or anyone really.

Mother would eventually attempt suicide.

As she sat before me, she didn't even know how to ask questions.

I turned over cards and read them as conversation. I watched her relax and let the words flow over her.

It was more like a baptism than a reading.

I described a blue sky she would see. And a blanket on the grass. And a distant stranger on the horizon.

Her face grew solemn.

And I laughed, "And now you're waving!"

I folded the cards, set them beside me, and sat smiling.

I refused her money when she offered.

She didn't know what to make of that. She sat back, thinking, looking at me. No one had ever given her anything. This was her first lesson in taking.

"Thank you," she said, her forehead thick with blush.

"Welcome," I said. "Nice to meet you."

CHAPTER 27

He was nineteen, she was seventeen. They'd come together on a lark. They wanted their fortunes told. Her first.

She had short hair with blond sideburns. She was a smiler.

He was dark, equine nose, with a blade of whiskers just working up from his jaw into his smooth cheek. Although he was smirking, I could tell he was honest. He wanted to see the cards.

Both wore the same jeans, but at least they had different shirts.

"What is it you want to know from the deck?" I asked.

They glanced sideways at each other and shrugged.

Often with couples like this, it's just predicting pregnancy and then wedding bells, or wedding bells and then pregnancy.

I always play along.

I laid out four cards and acted spooky.

I said, "I see a long white gown with small pearls and lace."

And then I pointed at the boy.

"And you're not wearing it."

That's always good for a laugh.

CHAPTER 28

Evil sat before me. He was 40, his face smiling, yet his eyes reserved. He was acceptably dressed, seemingly well-fed, in health. But there was a sense that he'd use good reasoning on you like a hammer.

He looked human. But behind the reasonable look of his face was a hardness and a resentment that was secretly waiting. And that at the right opportunity, it would strike or spit poison without provocation. It would simply strike at the first opportunity.

So what should I do? Oh, I could give a reading that tears his guts out. I could spread cards that open his chest, throw his heart out on the table, green, gelatinous, covering with squirming vermin. I could say, there look at it! And as his mouth opened, I watch as he begins banchee screams. But then I'd have the gelatinous mess on my hands.

So I simply take the easy way out.

"Sorry, closed today," I said happily, behind my mask of ire that evil has set foot in my shop.

Turning a monster back out on the street to do harm to others, tod hurt children.

And as the evil one nodded and left, easily redirected, I let the door shut.

And I turned over the Karma card. And I sneered at his back.

CHAPTER 29

So a woman in a polka-dot dress came in and asked me how many pink plastic flamingos she should put in her yard.

I turned over the Ten of Water.

"Ten," I said.

CHAPTER 30

Once I found this note on my chair:

"Oh, I do love you. As is your habit, you draw only the best cards for me. Each card is a gift, as each of your breaths is a gift.

Wind, water, fire, and earth. I love you in all elements.

I dress you in a black cape covered with all the symbols of the cards.

I see you standing out strong, your thoughts taking light like the Statue of Liberty looking into the Fourth of July night.

May the cards and the maker of the cards set their blessing upon you like a fiery crown.

Wherever I find you, love, is my good fortune."

It must have been one of my better readings. I never knew from whom.

CHAPTER 31

"What is your name?" I asked.

"Elenore," she replied.

"What is it you want to know?" I asked.

"Don't you know already?" she gibed. An old joke.

"A card reader reads what's in the cards. A soothsayer foretells the future," I said patiently, "You're sitting in front of a card reader."

"How does one become a card reader?" she asked.

"Like all things, you become educated in the art. And if it suits you, you become it. I studied at the U of G for several years."

"U of G?" she asked.

"University of Gypsy," I smiled.

Her eyes crinkled and she nodded amused. Her hair was the yellow-red of flames in a hot fire. She had a ruby so large you could mistake it for hard candy.

"Well, I was wondering..." she paused.

"If you're waiting for a drum roll, I don't think it's coming," I said.

We were starting to have a pretty good time.

Her lips parted and she laughed showing a happy crescent of white teeth.

"Has anyone ever read your cards?" she asked.

"Of course, as an apprentice with my teachers, I have had many readings. I read the cards for myself occasionally."

"Why only occasionally?" she asked.

"If you know what's in the cards..." I raised my shoulders and showed palms and wrists. The fastest explanation is none.

"What do you know about me?" she asked. At least she didn't flutter her eyelids.

"You like to reverse roles. Question the questioner," I said. "You like to control situations. You do this mainly with charm, and I wager also with astute intelligence. It's a tool. It keeps people at bay."

"Touché!" She sat back and laughed. Her hands dropped from the table and disappeared into her lap.

"Elenore," I said.

"Yes?" she said. She leaned forward as if at the opening curtain of an opera.

"Have you ever been deeply in love?" I asked.

"Yes, once," she said, thoughtfully, "But it wasn't my husband."

That was said plainly enough.

"You can love again, you know, if you're open to it," I said.

"What? With a card reader? Are you asking me for a date?"

"No, you mistake me," I laughed. "Elenore, relax. I'm not proposing."

"Thank God," she said. Her hands came up out of her lap, and the great candy ruby again shone on the table.

Without another comment, I turned over two cards. As I suspected the Seven of Wind and the reversed Two of Water.

"Don't let the mind's burden cut you off from your heart's desire," I said. "The two can co-exist. It is not war. It is life."

"I want to love," she said. It was a tone full of woe.

"You can," I said.

She left, after offering me her ring which I refused.

CHAPTER 32

My worst reading.

He was a bit portly, overly dressed, in a black tuxedo, blinding white shirt, and black bow tie. His wife, much smaller, practically mousy, was in a deep purple sack with black velvet shoes and spindle heels. It was late, nearly 10:30, and they'd dropped in on me on a whim after dinner out and the theatre.

He was offensively confident. I imagined if he'd had white gloves he'd have been pulling them off casually finger by finger before me.

A half-inch of gold pipe had been sawed off by some jeweler and jammed on his finger. His wife clung to his shoulder like a shadow.

"My name is Roger P. Thornton, and this is my wife, Jenny," he said.

"Glad to meet you," I said. The card reader should remain nameless.

"What would you like to know?" I asked.

"We'd like to ask all the important questions," he said blithely. By his tone I knew he expected no answers. This was an amusing stop on the way home.

"And you?" I asked, inclining to address his wife directly. Her eyes widened a bit that she'd been asked anything. Then her chin nodded in several small dips. She crossed her legs and put her hand on his elbow.

"Very well," I said.

I unwrapped my deck. I shuffled several times. I looked up, smiled, and sat silent.

Finally Roger came to and asked his first question.

"Will my stock portfolio grow beyond ten million?" he asked. He looked at his wife with a joshing rise of the eyebrows. She ducked her head and grimaced a smile at his good inside joke.

I turned over the reversed One of Earth.

"Disaster," I said.

He sniffed, then laughed.

"Well, then, about my business. We're looking at a merger, I'm to be bought out. I've just about rammed this deal through. I stand to make so much. I want to know will I sign the deal next week? Then we retire to Bimini, aye, Jenny?" He laughed; she smiled tightly in return.

He felt confident that his deal would go through.

I turned over two cards, the reversed Four of Earth and the chaotic Five of Earth.

"The deal fails, you may lose your job," I said.

"You mean the board of directors would vote me out?" he asked incredulous.

I turned over the reversed Wheel of Fortune.

"They may have already done so," I said.

He sat back and put his fingers to his lips. Then he came forward again laughing.

"What about my health, do I get to keep that?" He looked at his wife as he licked his lips.

I turned over the Three of Earth, The Hanged Man, and The Tower, all reversed.

"Bad news," I said. I shut up and didn't want to elaborate.

By now, his mouth was getting dry. Jenny was shrinking fast.

"At least you didn't pull the death card," he joked.

"The death card would have been better. It's a good card, one of transformation. These cards would be likely if you were to have a prolonged stay in a hospital." Then I bit my tongue. The cards were unloading here, and I had never delivered such news.

He swallowed. His forehead wrinkled, he hung a finger in his black bow tie to loosen it.

"Well, love conquers all," he rallied. He smiled fiercely at his wife, but he was bluffing now.

"We'll still have our love, always, won't we, Jenny?" Involuntarily my hand turned the next card. I couldn't believe I'd done it.

It was The Lovers, reversed.

He looked at the elegant card of two lovers entwined and smiled and said, "See!" His wife blinked and nodded, trying to smile.

"No," I said, "It's reversed."

"What!" His voice rose and he'd jumped up at the table.

"Jenny, have you been unfaithful?" He stood over her as she quailed in the chair alone. She only looked at him with her lips tight. Then she began to cry. She nodded.

I was ready to blow.

I laughed. And I couldn't stop laughing.

I found myself lying on my back on the floor, laughing, writhing, the cards scattered all over me. Finally, I sat up breathless. My eyes were wet.

I didn't even know they'd left.

CHAPTER 33

The rain on the shop window drips, meanders, runs like all the thousands of tears in the world.

Like all others, I simply build card houses and watch them fall down.

CHAPTER 34

The mystery of the cards is that they're spontaneous, uncontrollable, and synchronistic.

I might hazard a reason why, but it'd be unbelievable.

I can only say that once I did a reading for a woman who was having trouble at home. I drew four cards: the One, Two, Three, and Four of Earth, all reversed, all in a row.

I remarked to her the probability of drawing four cards in order from a shuffled tarot deck was highly unlikely.

I figured it at around 27 million to one.

It's like God coming along and tapping his finger on the top of your head and handing you a message.

It's all right if you haven't got much to say, just take the message.

CHAPTER 35

We were all bad people. She didn't like me and she didn't like her friend. She didn't have to say these things, she simply looked them at you. Her friend, a heavy woman, sat solemn faced with a two or three-foot space between them.

It was her friend who'd convinced her to have her cards read.

I asked her what she wanted to know.

Before answering, she sighed to signify this was all a waste of time.

When she looked at me, I noticed her eyes were almost the colorless hazel of shallow water. "Go on, Shawna," urged the friend, "ask a question. It can't hurt."

I realized the heart of this heavy woman next to her may have been divine. I cast a second look at her a moment.

"Okay. Why is the world like this? You know, all animals eating other animals?" she asked. Her jaw was stern with exasperation.

"I suppose," I said lightly, "Because some of those other animals just taste good. I serve them with various sauces."

Incensed that I'd made a foolhardy remark, she spat, "Well, why don't you just eat your lobster raw, Mr. Rich Man?"

"Because the lobsters don't like it and pinch you," I said. "They're better when you make them boiling mad."

"I know when I'm being made fun of!" Her teeth gritted. She winced up, readying to leave.

Her heavy friend slowly put out her hand and rested it on Shawna's angry wrist. She simply left her heavy palm on Shawna's arm, and the angry woman remained seated, then relaxed.

I'd never seen this: here was a woman with a healing touch.

I relented. It's not my job to reflect, but to read. I looked into her friend's brown eyes a long moment. She nodded ever so slightly.

"Shawna," I said, "What do you want to know?"

Shawna's face was pinched and red. She blinked tears onto her dress.

"I have cancer. I want to know if I'm going to die," she whispered.

I shuffled. I drew a breath and turned a card.

The Six of Earth: Glory.

"No, Shawna, I don't think so," I said. "Not with a friend like this one."

Shawna broke down and wept. She was enveloped quickly in the shawl of her friend's arm. Her friend helped her up and led her to the door.

When the friend turned to pay me, I shook my head. I merely lifted her hand and kissed it. And then I, too, felt tears brim.

THE FOOL

CHAPTER 36

"Are you open?" she called in sweetly. She was leaning in the door like a person looking out from a back stage curtain.

She had a crown of short blond hair and a half-twisted comical smile. In jeans, she wore a baggy deep purple sweater with nothing on underneath.

I picked her out as a student from the theatre school.

I put down my half-eaten sandwich and nodded, mouth full. Before I could clear my mouth she had seated herself at the table.

"I'm not catching you at your lunch hour or something?" she asked. She was hunched and leaning over the table now inspecting my sandwich. I had to sit back and smile.

"Would you like a bite?" I asked.

"Sure!" she said. To my surprise she reached forward and took up the untouched other half of my sandwich. She had two bites down and was nodding at its goodness to me when I had to laugh.

"Welcome," I said, "To my reading room. Should I read the cards or you?" I was amused.

"Oh, let's have you do it this time for once," she said with a theatrical backhand brush of feigned brusqueness.

She looked over my sandwich and smiled.

"My name is Beatrice, by the way, but people call me Betty."

"Charmed, enchanté, Betty."

"I'm sure," she said. Her eyebrows went up to signal that she would have laughed if she hadn't been chewing.

"What do you want to know?" I asked.

"Oh, tell me a good story," she said.

"My cards don't tell stories," I said.

"Why not?" She put down my sandwich and looked at me with inclined head.

"They're cards," I said. I shrugged.

"You mean people tell stories or something?" she asked.

"Yes," I said. "I suppose they do. Some good stories, some with happy endings, some not."

"Stories with ugly beasts, seven dwarves, and boys made of wood, and such, right?" she said.

"Those are fairy-tales, I'm talking about real stories," I said. "Real stories sometimes don't even have endings."

"Gotcha," she said. She smiled, because she didn't really have a clue, but she didn't care.

I laughed.

"So what's your pleasure," I said, lifting my card deck.

"Now you're talking," said Betty. She wiped an invisible mustache of crumbs from her lip.

"Have the cards tell me my story," she said.

"Betty!" I laughed, "The cards don't tell stories!" I shook my head, grinning.

“What do they do then?” she asked. She squinted at me, her mouth pulled aside. For the first time, Betty looked around my gypsy reading room taking in the furnished landscape with interest. I saw the clean white teacup of her ear.

“Betty, they tell the truth,” I said.

“Yeah sure,” said Betty, her sweater having slipped a bit to delightfully expose some bare shoulder. She smiled.

“Whatever,” I said. Just to have her look at me made me want to laugh.

I liked her. She was so bold and beautiful.

I spread 10 cards on the table for a long reading.

CHAPTER 37

“The Two of Water,” I said.

“The Two of Water signals a time of intimate connection. From the great potential of your heart, you reach out, you feel, you find. At start you are partially a fool, a lovely fool, but as if by magic, the connection is made. The truth is, in Nature’s abundance, you always find the thing you seek. And you seek an intimate connection with all things. These connections tell you who you are. You learn. You grow. Your heart becomes great, great with feeling, with generosity, with love, with the shining light of life for all around.”

“The Two of Water is a wonderful card to draw in the Spring. It is a bringing forth into form. New things arrive. Beauty unfolds. Pleasures emanate. You laugh with the pure white teeth of joy. You hear an old melody, very deep, buried in your heart."

"I sometimes believe," I said as an aside, "That the Two of Water is our salvation."

CHAPTER 38

"My goodness," said Betty, "It sounds like I'm going to have a good time."

I laughed, "You bet."

I then described the card.

"This card is called the Sacred Cord. Water, the realm of emotions, is opening to you.

"See the two cups? They are overflowing, bursting with the joy of clean water, refreshment, new life."

"Above the cups is a great new wave, a wave that threatens to overwhelm, rising to heaven, and there," I pointed at the figures floating at the card's top, "there, are the angels that guide you. Who welcome you to heaven's door."

"This card is a colorful thing. A thing of beauty."

Betty sat silent, looking at the cards, a strange smile upon her face.

Then she looked up at me.

"What is your name?" she asked.

"What?" I asked.

People almost never become social during a reading.

"You know my name. And you tell me these wonderful things. But I don't even know your name."

"Jean," I said.

"Nice to meet you, John," she said. She leaned forward, placing a cheek in the cup of her palm, her other arm extending a wrist and lank hand.

I quickly took her hand, squeezed, then dropped it. It had felt cool and creamy. I laughed in spite of myself.

"Not John, Jean, Jean Le Croix, my ancestors were French. My parents kept the old names."

"Shall we continue the reading?" I coaxed.

That brought up Betty's arm, pulling back her purple sleeve. After she'd exposed a wrist, she peered at a watch on a thin black leather band.

"Oh, I have a rehearsal! I have to go! Can we continue later? This is too good to stop."

"Of course," I said. "I'll write down the cards and I can finish when you return."

"Oh, thank you!" She reached out and patted my wrist. I was surprised that she'd touched me.

"My rehearsal is over at three. Back then. Okay?"

She stood, pulling her deep purple sweater up on her shoulder. She went to the door, took one step out, then turned, raised a hand half-cupped and made a small wave, biting her lips with pleasure, and left.

My goodness, I hadn't seen the tornado before it hit.

CHAPTER 39

I wrote down her cards. They were:

Two of Water: The Sacred Cord

The Water Mother

One of Fire: Force

Eight of Earth: The Mountain

Karma, reversed

The Tower

The Hanged Man

Five of Earth: the Nadir

The Wheel of Fortune

The Universe

I wondered if Betty would return for them.

CHAPTER 40

I walked down the street to McGregor's, the local florist. Pushing open the door, I was hit by the heady wall of scent from crowds of flowers in waiting. I nodded to Mr. McGregor behind his green counter.

"Afternoon, Mr. Le Croix," called McGregor. He was short, bald with shiny pate, and a green apron with straps over his shoulders. He was a smiling formal man; although invited several times, he'd never called me by first name. I'd been coming to his shop for 10 years.

He was expertly snipping rose stems. He put down his shiny clippers with the odd-shaped nose and laid his last rose, like a long candle, in a tissue-papered box. Today he had on a red tie under his apron.

"You received your scarlet Cyclamen?" he asked. The sleeves of his white shirt were rolled up as he leaned on one bare arm, hand flat on the counter. His other hand had wandered back to find the small of his back.

"Yes, they were quite a bush, very full. Thank you," I said. "This morning, I dropped them off at the Sisters."

"Nice of you as usual," said McGregor. He had an aging aunt at the Sisters of the Mercy a few blocks from my apartment house.

"So what's for today? Something blue?" He opened a fogged glass door and pulled a leafy cane of Iris. The ruffled plum flowers were large, floppy like dog ears. "These'll stand up a month. You could practically build a house with them."

I shook my head. "No something welcoming."

McGregor opened another fogged door. He reappeared holding what looked like a fire hydrant of white roses.

"I could stick these in a big brass cauldron. You could stow them in your fireplace. A wonderful surprise look."

"Perhaps something a bit more colorful?" I suggested.

McGregor went merrily to the next fogged panel. He enjoyed these problem solving games.

"Now here," he said, reappearing with his back to me. He turned around to reveal an arching spray of daisies, flower faces dyed brilliant colors and arranged in the ordered hues of a rainbow.

"Take a piece of the sky home with you," McGregor laughed.

"I think I will," I said.

"Would you like it delivered as usual?"

"No, I'll take it with me right now."

I picked up the huge bouquet and waddled toward the door as McGregor found a pencil and went to write on his tablet.

"Tomorrow, Mr. Le Croix," he called without looking up.

CHAPTER 41

I had just about made it back to the door of my shop when I heard a call behind me.

"Oh, my goodness are those for me?" She'd put her two hands together as if praying and was unabashedly mocking me.

I looked at her, holding the flowers at my chest.

I felt kind of foolish, the mysterious card reader exposing one of his foibles.

"I like flowers," I said.

"Betty," she said.

"Betty," I smiled.

"How did your rehearsal go? Are you in a play?" I hastened on.

"Oh, we stumbled through. As my final project, I have to create and perform a two-act piece."

I stood holding the flowers. Betty put her hands in her pockets.

"Well," I said, breaking the stalemate, "Come in, come in, we'll finish the reading..."

"Who are the flowers for?" Betty asked.

"Myself," I shrugged.

"You give flowers to yourself?"

"Yes."

"I like it when other people give me flowers, that's the best," she said.

"Other people can't always be counted on," I said, "I can. Coming in?"

"Not until you let me hold the flowers," she challenged. She was up to mischief.

I pushed the flowers into her chest and they hung beautifully there against her deep purple sweater.

Betty laughed.

I unlocked the door to my shop.

Betty came in close behind.

CHAPTER 42

When I closed the door and turned, I found Betty in front of me. She looked up at me and said, "I want you to kiss me."

"Why?" I asked.

"Because I want you to."

I looked at her blond hair, her clear blue eyes the color of dawn, her beautiful face open and willing.

I kissed her. Her hand touched lightly at my cheek.

"Mmm," she smiled, opening her eyes, "What card was that?"

CHAPTER 43

Betty put my flowers on the table. The spray seemed to leap like a fountain of color, like sky rockets. She stood looking at them an instant.

"Jolliette," she said.

She turned and saw my forehead wrinkled.

"Jolliette. Betty Jolliette. I know your last name, but you don't know mine."

"It's not often that you kiss someone before you even know their name," I said.

"I know. It's wonderful, isn't it?" Betty laughed.

"I think it is," I said.

"Much better than business cards," Betty said.

"If you saw my clients, you'd prefer business cards," I said, "But of course, you seldom give a card reader your business card."

"I wonder why," laughed Betty.

"Some think I already know the future, many aren't comfortable with that, they don't see me as a client, an investor, even a friend."

"You don't actually?"

"Oh, I learn their hearts," I said, "And when you learn that, you learn their future."

"You learn their hearts," repeated Betty smiling at me. "I think that's rather poetic."

"I suppose," I said.

Betty folded her arms in front of her and pinched her chin between two fingers like someone considering an easel.

"You know what?" she said finally, "I think those flowers were for me."

I laughed.

CHAPTER 44

"Have you had any lunch since you left here?" I asked.

"No," said Betty.

"Then let's go get you some."

"What about my reading?" she asked.

"I think we should continue that later," I said. Betty pulled up her purples sleeves and said, "Okay. Where to?"

"How about where all gypsies eat: McDonalds," I said. I watched Betty's eyes go questioning, then she caught my expression and laughed. She wasn't the only one handing out mischief.

"Of course gypsies eat at McDonald's," she said, "They have drive through."

I went and elbowed the door wide and waited for her.

She took my arm and we went out together.

"What about my flowers?"

"They're yours, Betty Jolliette, and no one can take them from you."

Betty shook her head and laughing said, "Weird."

CHAPTER 45

A red-haired girl walked by carrying a white-and-blue paper kite, dragging a long blue plastic tail snaking on the sidewalk behind her. She held the spindle of string like a candle as she walked.

It was warm and still. There was no wind.

"I wonder what she's doing with that?" questioned Betty.

"High pursuits," I said, "Matched by high ambitions."

"Do you always talk like that?" asked Betty.

I found her walking close beside, looking at me.

"Like what?" I asked.

"Oh, I don't know," she smiled, "Making elevated pronouncements about the everyday facts. Kind of pompously."

"As opposed to just walking up and kissing people?" I challenged.

That drew back the bow of Betty's white teeth.

"Well, yes," she said.

"I suppose it's a habit, from reading the cards. It's a kind of telegraphic, monologue approach to saying what needs to be said."

"Monologues, I understand those," said Betty, "Some actors love them. It gives you a chance to spout off, to be seen..."

"To star, to be applauded," I finished.

"Well, yes," admitted Betty. "But I find it boring. Talking to yourself, about yourself."

"You don't like the 'To Be or Not To Be' soliloquies?" I asked.

"I don't. I am," said Betty.

"And you are," I said. Then I laughed.

We were slowly walking the sidewalk around the park. There was an out-door cafe I had in mind. A yo-yo rolled out from a bush flapping its string across the sidewalk. A boy came leap-frogging after it. A radio fiddled a cheerful note from an open window. A teenager rode by tilted on the rear wheel of his bike. On a near bench, an old woman laughed and brushed at her hair as a pigeon attempted stubbornly to land there, while a lawn sprinkler hissed, spritzing the world in a long endless turn. It as an unexpected world.

"I prefer dual roles. Actors playing off each other," said Betty.

"I'm sure you do," I said. Betty sniffed, smiling.

We reached the cafe. A few tables with metal chairs were on the sidewalk.

"Let's try here," I said.

"Jolly good," said Betty. I squinted at her.

"I've been reading a lot of Shakespeare," said Betty. "My two-act project is a conversion of 'Much Ado About Nothing'. It's called "Too Much To Do About Everything."

"Sounds interesting," I said.

"And I'm the star," Betty said with over-the-top elevation.

CHAPTER 46

The cafe had a little rotisserie with cooked chickens circling and dripping under pink light. The place was empty because it was late afternoon. A waiter behind the counter with a bread-loaf chef's hat waved a knife at us and walked over. He stood and pulled his mouth to the side without saying a word. Coming inside, the place seemed dark, like stepping into a basement.

"Something?" the waiter finally said.

"Sure," I said.

"Go for it," said the waiter.

"Do you have any chicken?" asked Betty. She pointed at the rotisserie full of chickens.

"A few, mostly friends that I'm currently roasting behind me," said the waiter without blinking.

"What do you think?" I asked Betty.

"As long as they're friendly," said Betty.

"They were friendly, now they're roasted," corrected the waiter.

"I like your hat," said Betty.

"All the ladies do," said the waiter. "It makes my head look like mush."

Betty laughed.

"Shall we eat one of his friends?" I asked.

"Go for it," said the waiter.

Betty laughed and nodded.

"As long as he doesn't name names."

Betty said she'd like to eat outside in the park. I bought a chicken, cut into halves, and some bread. The waiter shook out a brown bag with a snap. He loaded two cones of French fries wrapped in newspaper into our bag of chicken and we were off, Betty stuffing a fistful of napkins into her jean's back pocket so that they hung out like a white tail.

At the door, Betty turned back with a small wave to the waiter.

"Come back again, I have a lot of friends," he called.

CHAPTER 47

As we traipsed into the park, bag in arms, Betty dug a few French fries out of the bag, stuffing them into her mouth, then handing me one of the lanky worms. I found Betty nodding and raising her eyebrows at me, signalling me they were good.

I motioned to an empty bench shaded by a tree beside a crowded flower patch. Orange birds of paradise were leaning on their stalks watching.

"No, let's eat over there," said Betty, clearing her chewing mouth and pointing at a small sunny grass knoll.

We walked to the top of the knoll and sat, surrounded by a meadow view of families kicking soccer balls, batting with badminton rackets, and skimming frisbees to children and jumping dogs. The normal park menagerie during sunny weather.

Betty opened the bag and peered in like Alice down the rabbit hole. She handed me a half chicken, then captured her own in her lap.

"This looks yummy," she said to her lap.

She picked up the half-chicken and bit in. She really wolfed it down. She was taking big bites and chewing hard.

"You eat like you mean it," I said.

"If you're expecting me to laugh and shoot chicken out my nose," Betty said shaking her head, gulping between bites.

She ate ravenously.

Finally she tore off a drumstick and waved it around the park like a conductor, coming up for air. "Sorry, people in my family have big appetites, even the dog."

"Do you have a big family?"

"I have four brothers. I'm the oldest. Did I make it sound like I come from a wolf pack? They aren't, not really. They're more sitters than wolves."

"You mean setters," I said.

Betty smiled and shook her head. "No sitters. My father is an Episcopal priest. We did a lot of sitting quietly in the pews. We were excellent sitters. We called ourselves "The Buns of Steel."

"My goodness," I said.

"You can imagine what happened when that nickname got around school. I still haven't forgiven my youngest brother."

"Betty, I'm starting to know too much about you," I said.

Betty laughed. She waved her drumstick chiding me.

"I bet you didn't see that in the cards," she said.

"Those types of things aren't in the cards," I said.

"And they shouldn't happen to anybody," Betty said between bites, inspecting her drumstick. Then she laughed.

CHAPTER 48

A bald-headed man sat down at the park bench by the flowers and opened a black case. He hung what looked like a huge toothpick in his mouth. After a few moments of picking up black tubes, he'd assembled an oboe. He fit the toothpick into the instrument's throat and brought the black stick to his mouth. He wiggled the keys experimentally.

I looked over to find Betty staring intensely at him.

The bald musician leaned forward with a deep calm breath.

A slow, lyrical melody began, a song to match the glide of butterflies. The man leaned as he played like a mast at sea.

"Lovely," whispered Betty.

"I hired him," I said stoutly.

Betty laughed and bounced her drumstick off me.

"Let's just listen a bit," Betty said.

"Okay," I said.

We sat together, on a grassy hill, in the Spring sunlight, and listened to unplanned, unforeseen music.

At one point Betty closed her eyes like a cat.

And the musician simply played. Played for all the unlistening and listening ears, the wandering animals, the play field and runners, the leaning flowers, played for the leafy shade, the high sun, the sky in its comfortable neighborhood of white clouds, the laughter of children, the bees prospecting deep inner blossoms, the hummingbirds' business-like skimming, the panting dogs, the ducks waddling, and the slow curving cement paths everyone walks.

He played music for it all. And that's all. When the song ended, I found Betty smiling with her hand on my arm.

"It makes me want to stand up and do cartwheels," she said.

And then she stood up and did a cartwheel.

CHAPTER 49

Betty reseated herself.

"I haven't done that in years," she said.

"I haven't done that," I said.

"Never?" she asked.

"Well, perhaps as a kid, but I never remember any in which I actually went all the way over. More roll and plop."

"I have native cart-wheel intelligence," said Betty. "I could teach."

"No, I think not. I'm much too old for that."

"How old would that be?" asked Betty.

"Old," I said. "Older than some trees, younger than most rocks."

"I'd say you're in your thirties," guessed Betty.

"Twice your age," I said. Betty laughed.

"Now that's a compliment, how old do you think I am? I'm twenty-two! That'd make you forty-four."

"Sorry, I thought you were a theatre student getting your BA."

"MFA, my project's for my Masters."

"Betty," I laughed, "What does age have to do with it? I don't really see why we're having this conversation."

"No reason really," said Betty shrugging, giving me a sly look. "It's just most often it's age that kills you."

"I thought it was the hardening of something," I said.

"Yes, the hardening of the heart," finished Betty.

"In deed so," I said. "That's in the cards."

CHAPTER 50

The oboist had begun his second song, this one more noted and classically technical than the first, when a heavy woman, one I'd characterize as an oblivious rhinoceros, walked up and sat on the bench. When she sat, the musician's case bumped sideways. She sat in a heavy gray sweater lower than her waist, in blue pants whose legs might have been chimneys, digging into a small pouch on her lap. The woman took out two packs of cigarettes, one the familiar beige and tan of Camels, the other a green mentholated brand. She pulled a cigarette from each pack and put two in her mouth. She lit both, lifting one at a time with her lips for the flame, then dropped her lighter back in the pouch. She took down one cigarette as she drew in heavily on the other.

By now the oboist, askance, had picked up his case and fled.

The obese woman sat alternately smoking one cigarette then the other. She stared off sourly.

Betty and I watched amazed. She was a smoke stack.

Finally, I said, "She must be cutting down, normally she's a three pack person."

CHAPTER 51

Betty and I began to walk back toward the shop. I was carrying the leftovers of our outdoor meal in a grease-blotched bag.

"Thanks again for lunch," said Betty. "It was great. I should make it a habit."

"My pleasure," I said.

"Do you come out into the park much?"

"You mean do I walk here? I was born here, my mother took me here all the time. As a kid, I buried things out in that grass, treasures, you know, the kind you dig up later? They're probably still out there. Hard to find." I waved an arm at the expanse of grass.

"Did you make maps with an X?"

"Yes, pirate maps, and I even burned holes in them to make them look authentic."

"What did you bury?"

"Oh, keys without locks, marbles, a box of matches, real treasures."

"What did you do with the maps?"

"Oh, I lost them too," I said, shrugging.

We were now within a block of my shop in a bushy lane. High eucalyptus held up the sky behind us.

And there on the sidewalk was a fish.

Betty's sharp eyes saw the goldfish on its side some fifteen feet ahead.

As we approached, it turned into a C, then lay flat.

"It's alive!" cried Betty.

I looked down at the fish wide-eyed and gasping. With nary a drop of water anywhere in the vicinity. "I wonder..." I began when Betty jumped forward.

She scooped up the little fish and ran. She disappeared left off the path into the bushes. I was obliged to jog behind her to keep her in sight.

"Betty?" I yelled.

Betty was running full out, holding the tail between two fingers, the fish wagging in the air like an improbably small gold purse.

Betty could run like a deer.

I could barely keep her in view as she plunged over a little rise of grass and down again.

As I made the rise, I saw Betty now dashing across the last fifty yards of grass to a sailing pond where kids and adults sailed model boats via string and remote control.

She slowed only when she reached the concrete edge of the pond, and then raised an arm, and the fish flew and hit the water with the smallest splat.

As I walked up behind Betty, she reached down and washed her hands. I could see her chest pumping.

She turned and said, "I think I made it."

"I think you just invented the goldfish relay race," I said.

CHAPTER 52

I looked questioningly at the sailing pond. "Do you think that's a long term solution?" I asked.

"When it's a question of survival, everything is short-term," sighed Betty.

"I suppose that's why survivalists are such bad planners," I said.

Betty looked at the pond a moment, it's flat water, no sign of life.

"Do you think we travelled here from the stars?" she asked the water.

"You mean in an astronomical relay race through space?"

"Yes."

I looked at her, admiring a mind that could think such a thought.

"Yes," I said, "guided here by the Goddess Betty."

CHAPTER 53

Pulling up her purple sleeves, Betty sat down on the concrete edge of the pond. She clasped her hands in her lap and blinked at me.

"You're nice to me," she said.

I sat down beside her. I was careful not to brush against her. For some reason I didn't want my shadow to fall on her.

"Good deeds," I said, "You're a doer of good deeds."

"I'm a doer," nodded Betty. "If you come from a family of my background, long sermons, and waiting, you get antsy to do things."

"Yes, I remember your creed, Buns of Steel."

Betty laughed, "I shouldn't have told you."

"You'll have to forgive your little brother now," I said.

"Yes, I guess so, since we both have sinned."

"Of course, I don't believe a damn thing about sin. That's just my father talking."

"Sounds like the religion washed off," I said.

"Years ago." Betty sat smiling at her hands, then she gripped them. "But of course, not the eternal," she peered at me, "I don't want you to think I'm shallow."

"Betty, the saver of fish, shallow? Who could think it?" I said.

"I don't want you to is all," said Betty.

"The eternal is in the cards, and the cards are always in you," I said.

"There you go again," smiled Betty. "Being complimentary in total weirdity. Did your mother feed you too many wise foods, carrots and stuff?"

"We lived entirely on prunes," I said.

Betty laughed.

"So did half my father's congregation."

"Now I'm feeling just really good," I said.

"Oh, sorry. Here you're so complimentary to me and I'm likening you to a prune-eater."

"I started it," I confessed.

"Tell me more about the cards," Betty said, trying to repair things.

"They represent things inside us all, kind of a map of our inner space, you can use them to look inside yourself."

"What do you see when you look inside yourself?"

"You mean other than a big heap of prunes?"

Betty laughed.

"The cards have an ancient history. They tell us who we are and what we could be. They're very hopeful."

"How can shuffling cards and drawing them from a deck tell you all that?

"Because, all that is really inside you, the cards let it out."

"It's mysterious," said Betty.

"And prune-based," I said.

We laughed a bit, Betty raising a finger like a mustache to her lips. She tapped the side of her head to my shoulder then sat up.

CHAPTER 54

We looked left to find a young man in yellow shirt, green shorts, and sockless tennis shoes calling. Thin-faced, he had wire-rim glasses and a fuzzy goatee.

"Heya, Betty! You okay?"

"Andy, what are you doing here?" asked Betty.

"I saw you running across the park, with that guy after you," he said. "I didn't know what was up. "

"So you waited over there in the bushes to find out?" laughed Betty.

"Yes, I didn't know," admitted Andy. The young man, dressed for Summer on the first day of Spring, came up and stood before us. He was holding his shoulders in a sheepish angle.

"This is Andy McKenna," said Betty, "Andy, this is Jean."

"Heya," said Andy. He made a tight smile and shuffled his feet.

"Nice to meet you," I said.

"Andy lives across the hall in my apartment house. We had an undergraduate theatre class together."

"I'm her watchdog," said Andy. "I watch out for her apartment, and water her plants and stuff."

"And bark at strangers," finished Betty.

"Betty," complained Andy grimacing.

"What do you do?" asked Andy, raising his hairy chin at me.

"Even worse," I said, "I'm a card reader."

Andy's face went blank, unsure if he was being made fun of.

"I read Tarot cards," I said.

"He's a gypsy king and he has five wives," stated Betty.

Andy shrugged. "Don't worry about her, she treats everybody that way." He said this trying to reassure me, but there was another small inflection in it as well. A slight disappointment.

"Andy is in my final project. He plays Birddog, the saver of Virginity. Half the play he growls at women to keep them in line."

"I'm sure he growls with exquisite finesse," I said.

"Damn straight," said Andy. Then he smiled, his fuzzy goatee hanging like a loose birdnest.

"You really are a fortune-teller?" asked Andy. He put his hands into his back pockets for a talk.

"How do you do it?" asked Andy. Betty frowned, but I smiled it was okay.

"I suppose it's like learning lines," I said, "Turn a card, the scene is set, say your lines."

"I am the Great Swami and I foresee you paying me big bags of money," incanted Andy.

Betty laughed.

"Huge bags," I said, "I always say huge bags."

CHAPTER 55

Andy sobered. "We have that call in an hour. Are you still going with me?"

"Yeah," said Betty. Betty's head turned to me, "They're auditioning for a commercial downtown. Some extras and a couple-line part. I'm giving Andy a ride."

"Sounds interesting," I said. "Do you both do a lot of commercials?"

Andy shrugged, "Not me, though I did some voice-overs last year."

"Andy was Billy the Pea Pod," said Betty.

"Idol of worship of the seven-year-old set," admitted Andy.

"Billy the Pea Pod?" I said. "Can I have the autograph now?"

"Sure, as many as you want, ten bucks a throw. I'm a professional," said Andy regally. "Betty owes me thirty bucks."

"He pays the money he owes me with checks that bounce. He says the autographs are worth it."

"Fascinating," I said. "What is this commercial about that you're trying out for?"

"Kitty litter liners," said Andy.

Betty rattled her whole body, like a dog shaking off water, laughing.

"Tell him the one line," she said.

Andy made a fist, and with strong arm forward, said in a Tony-the-Tiger growl, 'They're GREAT!"

"My god," I said.

Betty was cawing, holding her sides laughing.

CHAPTER 56

"Are we going?" asked Andy.

Betty looked at Andy then to me. "I'll catch up to you in about fifteen minutes," said Betty.

Andy looked at her and nodded. He shrugged and turned to go, but then he stopped and nodded at me. Finally he left, his face holding a small grimace of disappointment.

"Well, I guess I have to go," said Betty.

"Fun lunch," I said.

"Wasn't it!" said Betty.

We sat a moment in silence.

"Can I come back to your shop sometime and finish my reading?"

"Certainly," I said.

"Good, I'd like that."

"What about my flowers?" said Betty suddenly.

"Another good reason you'll have to come back."

"Well, I will then," said Betty. "I'll get those flowers even if I have to break down the door."

"I'm sure," I said.

"And I can," said Betty making a fist and putting a strong arm forward.

"Buns of Steel," I said.

CHAPTER 57

I sat on the edge of the sailing pond, watching Betty retrace her steps over the grassy rise, leaving the park. I felt a bit abandoned and isolated. Perhaps like the little fish behind me.

CHAPTER 58

Helga came in for her reading. She was lonely and old, and the first thing she did was open her purse and hand me a dollar. It was scuffed and limp like a hanky. She always liked to make some payment on the money she owed me. She probably owed me a small fortune. She'd been coming for years. She always paid a dollar.

"Helga, how are you?" I asked.

"Lovely flowers," said the old woman looking at the rainbow of daisies set against the wall. "You must have found someone. Someone exciting." Her cheeks tightened and underneath the wrinkles was a smile.

"Next you're going to start charging me for readings," I said.

Helga raised a wizen forefinger and shook it at me in hammer taps.

"Young man," she warned, "No one needs cards to know how Spring works."

I laughed.

I unwrapped the deck for our normal session and cards that were always good.

At the end of the reading Helga sat back and closed her eyes as if at a séance. She told me she remembered her first husband gave her daisies when she was eighteen.

"When was that, about two years ago?" I asked.

Helga put her hand on my wrist and shook it as she cried.

CHAPTER 59

A funny thing happened that night. As I was watching TV, a commercial for kitty litter liners came on and my eyes sharpened to see if I could see Betty.

CHAPTER 60

The next day, I did several readings. I remember looking up several times during a session thinking I'd seen a purple sweater in the window.

The woman sitting in front of me noticed me lift my chin as I looked up from her cards. She said, "What is it? Something good?"

CHAPTER 61

And those flowers just sat there, aggravatingly happy.

CHAPTER 62

At the end of the day, I decided to close up shop.

My door doesn't have a bell that sounds when visitors enter, but the hinge is dry, so it makes a high violin squeal when opened. There'd been no violin announcement that day. I looked at the flowers. I resisted the urge to fool with them.

They were no longer mine. But I decided I was going to have to take them home.

I went to the door to look up and down the street one last time. No one. Just our local crazy lifting garbage can lids and looking in, his face as intent as any man at an expensive hotel buffet. He was wearing a black ski cap, haggard clothes, and hole-ridden army socks without shoes. His name was Wally and his speech was like a phonograph slowed down.

"Wally, you need a dollar?" I called.

Wally looked up from his can and watched me blinking.

"No," he said shrugging. He went back to picking through the sticky refuse.

I walked up to him and held out five dollars. I stood holding out my hand with its paper feather between my fingers.

Wally looked at me, frowned, and threw a dismissing hand.

"I don't need thaaaat hassle," he said.

He turned his back. I looked at him a moment.

Exclusive, Wally no longer accepted cash or visa.

CHAPTER 63

That night, out of pity for myself, I drew a card: The Hanged Man.

This usually signals an awkward period of waiting, suspension, eventual renewal.

That made sense.

CHAPTER 64

The next day, I gave Mrs. Johnson a reading. A carrot-haired woman, she chatted away as usual as I turned her cards. Most people sit silent and listen. But Mrs. Johnson had to talk, she'd even comment on a newly turned card before I could speak.

"Oh my, that's a nice one," she said, seeing The Moon and its beautiful maiden's face, and the mysterious animals below it, the wolf, the crab, creatures of the dark. All below a shining moon.

I looked out my shop window. Empty sidewalk.

"It's about the dark intuitive self. A place of safety and guidance on a journey."

"Am I going to take a trip? I loved Kauai!" laughed Mrs. Johnson.

"The journey is one of the soul toward another," I said.

"Ah, a new love!" sighed Mrs. Johnson. She was 56 and divorced three times.

I smiled tightly, "Lucky you."

She chatted on about her last lover who was a taxi cab driver who wanted to make love to her in his trunk.

"That was a journey in itself!" laughed Mrs. Johnson.

CHAPTER 65

Tuesday came. Wednesday went. Thursday dawdled. Friday widened.

CHAPTER 66

I parked my half-filled shopping cart. Down the aisle, two kids were throwing a bag of potato chips like a football between them. An old woman, who had opened an egg carton as carefully as a menu, had just taken out an egg and dropped it on the floor.

I'd quit early to do some after-work shopping. I often imagined you could find all of America lurching through Safeway Friday night, plunging our carts down the aisles like bumper cars in a feeding frenzy. Me, I didn't need much, just one or two things.

I stopped at the cantaloupes in the fruit section. I was alone, holding the bald spheres to my nose to remember their strong fragrance.

I felt a nudge at my elbow.

"No kissing the cantaloupes, Sir."

"Pardon?" I said, turning holding two melons at my chest.

There was the purple sweater and Betty cocking her head with fine white teeth, laughing.

"Are they good?" she asked.

"We just met, I don't really know," I said. I felt a strange crawling in my chest for her.

'Betty," said Betty. She pushed up her purpled sleeves like a card dealer going to work.

"Oh, I remember," I said.

"Sorry I didn't come by to finish my reading. Do you still have the flowers for me?" Betty asked.

"I have them," I said. Then I shrugged, "But they're not the same. The waiting. You know."

"I still want them," smiled Betty.

"I'm glad," I said.

Betty took a cantaloupe from my hand and sniffed it. She exchanged it for the other melon, sniffed, and gave it her blessing, saying, "This one."

"You'll have to come by to pick them up," I said. I put the melon in my shopping cart.

Betty looked about and picked up three apples. She tossed them into the air and did several flawless juggling passes.

"Theatrical people are required to juggle," she said, looking up at the fruit she was busily flinging.

Bright-eyed, she smiled as she juggled.

"I basically divide the world into two categories of people: Theatre people and me," I said.

Betty laughed and said, "Watch out. Low opinions hold you back."

Betty caught the three apples against her chest and put them back in the pile.

"Is that your Father the religious leader talking?"

"Heavens no, to him sinners all. That's theatre people wisdom," said Betty.

"See. Theatre people wisdom. That's not in the cards for me. At least I'm not required to juggle."

"No, but you do card tricks," challenged Betty with a raised eyebrow.

"Readings," I corrected with a magnanimity that was nearly majestic.

"Don't you think it's the same abracadabra, putting on a show?"

"No, I don't," I said. "I think there's a difference."

"I, as a theatre person, would say it's just a different role, one less played, but still a role."

"Theatrical people are like that: they portray things. I, on the other hand, like to peer deeply into cantaloupe to understand their inner natures."

"I looked through the window into your shop," said Betty, "The flowers weren't there."

"I took them home," I said.

"You don't live there?" asked Betty.

"No, I live about eight blocks from here."

"Great," said Betty, "Let's go get them."

"I don't have a car," I said.

"I'll help you carry the groceries," said Betty. Smiling, she had shoveled her two hands into her hip pockets and was standing with her back arched, breasts out. I realized with surprise that I had already kissed this person.

"Miss Helpful," I said.

"If you want," laughed Betty, "You could get in the cart and I could push you home."

"Well, I just might," I said.

CHAPTER 67

Ten minutes later we were both walking with groceries bags sealed to our chests. A huge moon hung in the horizon like a grapefruit. I could hear birds rattling around in the evening trees. The traffic and city had stilled with the last twilight. As we walked a bushy section around the park the great yellow orb cast faint shadows on the grass. The trill of tree frogs held its high string in the air. An occasional car passed as we lugged the groceries toward home.

"Sorry I didn't come back the other day," said Betty.

"Oh, no problem," I said.

"Complications," said Betty. "I had to deal with someone."

"Boyfriend?" I asked.

"Well, not anymore. He just doesn't believe it."

"Sorry to hear that."

"It happens. He's so tremendously egocentric. I'm not going for it. Problem is he's in my final project."

"So you can't get rid of him because you need him as an actor."

"Something like that."

"You can't recast?"

"My project is two weeks away. We have final rehearsals this week. One tonight in fact."

"That could be ugly for a kissing scene," I said.

"I suppose I could rewrite and make it so he has to kiss Andy," Betty laughed.

I remembered Andy as the youth in goatee and glasses from the park.

"By the way, did you get the part in the commercial you were trying out for?" I asked.

"No, but Andy did," said Betty, "He'll be the new spokes cat for the kitty litter liner company. He has to dress up in a cat suit for the commercial. He has four lines. And some acting."

"Acting?" I said.

"He has to root around in a gigantic cat box full of litter," said Betty.

"And there's acting in that?" I asked.

"Oh yes," she said, "He has to act happy."

Betty laughed.

We walked on in silence for several paces.

"You dumped your boyfriend," I said, "Did you find someone new?"

"Yes," said Betty looking straight ahead.

She hoisted her shoulders and said nothing more.

CHAPTER 68

We were within a block of my apartment house. I asked Betty if she was carrying the groceries okay.

"Sure. I'm pretty strong," said Betty.

"Have you been interested in acting long?" I asked.

"Oh, since I was a kid. It got me in trouble once in high school."

"How so?" I asked.

"You want the dirt, huh?" laughed Betty.

"It just makes for more accurate readings," I said in excuse.

"I come from a small town. Each year they have a Harvest festival. Main street sets up with street vendors, the carnival comes, we have a little parade. A small town celebration, you know? People come from miles around and jam the sidewalks for a day. The street vendors sell photographs, art, knickknacks, candles, cassettes, you name it. People walk up and down the closed-off street gawking at goods in booth after booth. A street fair, you know?"

I nodded.

"So I was in high school, and wanting to be an actor, in the school play and all."

"Did something go wrong in school?" I asked.

"Oh no. Not in school. Something went wrong at this fair, though. I was walking along when I came to a booth full of wooden toys. There was this angry fat woman standing in front of it, glaring down at her little boy. He was maybe four, in shorts. He as unhappy and he started crying because he wanted something. People were getting out of their way, clearing a path around them on the sidewalk."

"Well, this fat woman yelled at the boy to stop crying, then she slapped him. A real good smack."

I glanced left just in time to see old consternation pass across Betty's forehead.

"And?" I said.

"For a second, I was shocked. I just stood there. Then, I don't know why I did it, but I grabbed my face and yelled. I started screaming at this woman, 'Why'd you hit me? Why?' I just screamed away acting hit. And then I yelled for the police."

"I made a really big scene."

"A humongous crowd gathered. I kept yelling, the fat woman just standing there, going 'No, I didn't, I didn't hit her! She's crazy!' And in no time a policeman shows up to stop what's going on."

"What happened?"

"The policeman faces me and says, 'Okay, okay, what's up?'"

"I'm kind of out of breath from yelling. And there's a big crowd, you know? So I point at the woman and say 'She hit me!'"

"And she sputters 'No, I didn't! She's crazy, Officer!'"

"And then I say in a big astonished voice, 'Oh! You're right! Now I remember, you didn't hit me! You hit him!' And I pointed at the kid, whose face now has a bright red starfish on his cheek."

"Good for you," I said.

Betty shook her head.

"Oh, the officer, he was completely mad. He told me to mind my own business and to take off. And he told the woman to watch what she did to her kids and told her to take off. He waved the crowd off and we all went away."

"And that was it?" I asked.

"No," said Betty.

"Two weeks later, my father got a subpoena about a law suit that was filed against me and my parents. Defamation of character."

"What?" I said, my eyes crinkling.

"Oh, boy, was I in trouble," shrugged Betty. "My father couldn't understand what'd made me do it."

"What happened? Did you end up in court?"

"My dad talked to one of the men in his congregation. A city prosecutor. He let it be known that if this suit was pursued, he'd press for child abuse charges. The woman's lawyer would have to argue that although the woman slapped her own kids, it was a lie that she would slap a high schooler. It would make her look bad, like a coward. And the abuse thing scared her. So they dropped the suit."

"My first big street performance. Applause," sighed Betty.

I put my hands together in silent clapping.

I nearly dropped my grocery bag.

CHAPTER 69

"Oh, they look lovely," said Betty.

She stood looking at the rainbow flower spray set on a varnished maple end table against a white wall. Above it hung the rich tropical colors of my Gauguin. Unseen track lighting held all in an alter-like pose.

I put down my grocery bag on the bar counter, saying "My florist has the heart of an artist."

"I like that," said Betty. She glanced around taking in the prim modern furnishings of chrome and glass, stuffed chairs, wooly white throw rugs.

"Quite the place," she said uneasily. "What do card readers make anyway?" This last held a touch of disbelief.

"The pay isn't the money," I said.

"Someday, when I make it, and I've made my movies and such, I'll do this."

"That's good," I said, "But you're here now."

Betty nodded looking about the corners at several other floral arrangements from previous days.

"You like flowers," she said. Her hands were searching up and down her thighs uneasily for her pockets.

"Would you like some tea, Betty?" I asked, "I don't get many guests like yourself."

"Really?"

"You're the first in months," I said, "I often see too much of people during the day, and so at home I remain kind of isolated. Few visitors."

"I want big audiences to come and see me," said Betty.

"There we're different," I said. I stepped into the kitchen and began to wrestle water into a kettle. Betty came in close behind.

"Somehow I imagined your apartment to be more like your shop. A bit run-down but comfy, you know?"

"It's not comfy here?" I asked, holding a cold water kettle poised over the stove.

"Oh, it's comfy. But upscale and comfy. Not like the shop," said Betty.

"My shop is for my clientele. It makes them feel at home."

"I know I did," said Betty with just a hint of puzzlement.

"Earl Grey, Chamomile, Peppermint?" I asked.

"Peppermint," said Betty.

"Of course," I said.

CHAPTER 70

I handed Betty her tea in white china. She was sitting uncomfortably slouched in my low white couch. She nodded accepting the tea in her cupped hands like accepting a wafer at church.

I sat in the chair across from her gingerly holding hot tea over my lap.

"Do your clientele, do they ever become your friends?" asked Betty.

"No, rarely," I said.

Betty sat silent a moment.

"Why?"

"Oh, they come to me as something of an oracle. They aren't comfortable with that. They suppose I know more than I should know."

"Oracle, you mean a high-falutin' fortune-teller? Do you know more about them, more about their futures than they should know?"

"No," I said.

"So, do you lie to people, tell them things so they think they know their future?"

"No," I said.

"Well, what do you do then? Reading their cards?"

"It's hard to understand, but I teach simple lessons about what human beings are inside. And people recognize it in themselves. They see something they've forgotten or didn't know."

Betty gave up sitting uncomfortably on the sofa and slid down to sit Indian-style on the rug. She pulled her tea toward her across the glass topped table.

"I can't say that I get that," said Betty, "Do you have any sugar?"

"Sure," I said, getting up.

Retrieving the sugar from the kitchen, I called, "It's primitive psychology, that's one way to think about it."

"How is a card psychology? Thanks," said Betty, accepting a pink bowl of sugar cubes.

"The cards are a map of who we are inside. We have emotions, thoughts, spirit, our physical self, we go through periods of change. We transition from one thing to another. Just like people for thousands of years before us."

"My first grade teacher once talked about our hairy ancestors. So I thought I had an ancestor named Harry," said Betty.

I laughed.

"So how do the cards fit in?"

"They're symbols of those things, archetypes, human fundamentals that the ancients, whoever they were, probably your ancestor Harry, collected into a body of knowledge. I teach what the cards represent. And although it's primitive, it's better than nothing. Better than having no map to the self. Am I boring you?" I laughed.

"Nope," said Betty.

"Anyway, when people have a problem, are blocked from their future, it's often that they are blocked from parts of themselves. They've forgotten, ignored, or refused parts of themselves. Or they don't realize the next step in a natural transition that humans often make. I can't really put a zipper on it, but that's what I do."

"So, you tell your clients about parts of themselves, and then they can see their future?" asked Betty.

"Hopefully. Sometimes they just see themselves or see the now."

"But for the blind even that's wonderful," laughed Betty.

"Bright girl," I said.

"It makes me think back to my Greek Tragedy classes and catharsis," mused Betty.

"I think the great scenes, great actors, the great roles, do something of what I do," I said.

"What's that?" asked Betty.

"They portray what's in the cards," I said.

CHAPTER 71

"No way. You mean like the Wizard in the Wizard of Oz represents something from the Tarot?"

"The Emperor," I said, shrugging.

"Catherine Hepburn in The African Queen?"

"Temperence," I said calmly.

"Clark Gable in Gone with the Wind?

"The Wheel of Fortune," I said.

"Mickey Mouse and Pluto?" challenged Betty, her eyebrow raised merrily.

"The Fool and his dog," I laughed.

"James Bond?"

"The Magician."

"Tarzan?"

"Strength."

"Godzilla?"

"The Tower."

"Arnold Swartzeneggar saying 'Hasta La Vista, Baby.' Clint Eastwood saying 'Make my day'?" riposted Betty sliding into each actor's accent.

"The Five of Fire, the Five of Earth," I said.

Betty laughed.

"The Blue Fairy in Pinnochio?"

"The Heirophant."

"Romeo and Juliet?"

"The Lovers," I said. I sipped from my tea.

Betty looked at me and hesitated. She blinked three times and looked away.

CHAPTER 72

"Well," said Betty smiling and casting her eyes, "I told you about my brush with the law. Have you ever had any, as a card reader?"

"Yes," I said. "Nothing serious."

Betty tilted her head with the slightest shake, egging me on.

"Well, I'd decided to try reading in a small town. I thought there'd be more privacy. I didn't realize it was a small town with a big church."

"The first person through my door was the pastor."

"He sits down in his collar and says, 'Good morning, I'm Reverend John Ashburough, and I'd like a reading.'"

"I greeted him and threw a card."

"As soon as he saw the card, he jumped up as if threatened. His face expanded like a red balloon and he started yelling."

"What card was it?" asked Betty.

I shrugged.

"The Devil."

"He yelled, 'You think that's funny? Here we fight against the Devil!'"

I said, 'For me, the Devil is just a part of the deck, part of who we are.'"

"He huffed and left."

"That afternoon I had a dozen people standing outside my shop with pentacles painted on placards."

"They were chanting things like 'Go, Devil, go!"

"Whoa," said Betty. "Did they mob you?"

"No, no. But you see if you spend your whole time fighting against the Devil, that's how he likes to be worshiped. You're working at his feet."

"So what did you do, offer to start devil worship classes and invite them in?"

"I don't think so," I said in a pinched voice.

"Besides they wouldn't have understood."

"For the Tarot, The Devil represents our ability to have fun, to bend the rules, to be childish, a little devil, and also the ability to break rules in a big way if necessary. For example, in a war you may have to kill to survive. This devil is a force, a black part of us, without it you can't achieve for yourself, or even build a house."

"What did you do?" asked Betty, brow furrowed.

"Oh, I just left town," I said. "You see the card shows a smiling devil, holding his scepter, and at his feet are a man and a woman in chains. But if you look closely the chains are so loose, the man and woman could just step out of them."

"It means you can escape this devil whenever you want."

CHAPTER 73

"Your father ever run an exorcism of the local soothsayer?" I asked.

"Oh no, he always said you have to believe in a pretty bad God to believe in a pretty bad Devil."

"Then he'd kind of shrug and say, 'Besides, I have these kids.'"

I laughed. Betty smiled at me running a comb of three fingers through her short bangs. I could see from her eyes she liked entertaining me.

CHAPTER 74

Betty asked for a tour of my apartment. I walked her from room to room, my dining room with its glass top table and a turtle of blue pansies, my kitchen, my study with its large mahogany desk, a left-over from my father and his business life.

"Your father left that to you? It's practically an airport. Did he have a big office? What business was he in?"

"Captain and pirate of industry," I said. "All action, mergers, and raids. Many types of businesses, some legal, some not so."

Betty looked at me with a sideways glance, taking from my tone all this was not so happy with me.

"Laundry," I said, pointing an elbow at a closed hallway door.

Betty pushed forward and actually peeked in the laundry room. There stood the two white machines, resolute and sparkling.

"What did you expect, an avalanche of clothes?" I asked.

"I didn't see any dirty clothes at all," accused Betty.

"You think I wear them once and burn them? No, rest assured, it's all in knowing the proper technique for hiding dirty laundry under the bed."

"I'm going to check!" challenged Betty. She skipped off down the hall to the only door left unopened.

She entered my bedroom.

I came to the doorway. Betty was standing looking uneasily around. Like my livingroom, my bedroom was clean, bed with white bedspread evenly laid, white rug, no unruly clothes left in sight. Lamps with beige shades. A hanging plant of Wandering Jew, strings of bushy vines reaching toward the window.

“Everything is so neat!” said Betty suspiciously.

“The bed looks like you’ve never slept in it.” Betty ran a flat hand along the spread.

“I don’t sleep in it, I levitate a foot above it,” I said.

Betty’s mouth opened with disbelief.

I laughed.

“Betty, I have maid service,” I said. “Today was the day the maid came.”

Betty laughed and balled her hands up in her sweater. She shrugged having trouble looking at me.

“I just thought maybe you were a real weirdo,” she laughed uneasily.

“Then I don’t think you’d better look under that bed,” I cautioned.

“Why?” accused Betty playing along.

“Why? What’s under there?” she asked.

“Uncle Harry,” I said.

“You,” growled Betty.

CHAPTER 75

I asked and again discovered Betty was famished. I walked her into my kitchen and began putting together a meal, omelettes followed by spaghetti, at Betty’s request.

Betty pushed up her sweater sleeves to chop onion, warning me she needed to leave by nine.

"I have a rehearsal for my project," said Betty.

"Why so late?" I asked, stirring a solution of eggs and milk in a bowl.

"All the school's projects come due about the same time. There's a big demand on stage time."

"This play is important to you?" I asked.

"I mess it up and I don't get my MFA. I end up staying another semester," said Betty, busy chopping. "I intend to be in New York this summer, looking for parts."

"New York in summer? Won't you have to bring a fireman's jacket for the heat?"

"Oh no," smiled Betty, "Not for people who live in the subway. They never see the light of day."

"Agreed," I said.

"Do you plan to do that? Live in poverty in New York as you look for work?"

"Sure. Haven't you read your 'How To Become a Famous Actor' manual?"

"I guess not," I said.

"Rule #2: Throw yourself at all directors so that they can claim to discover you."

"Throw yourself? You'd really throw yourself at people?" I asked.

"What, you mean sexually?" laughed Betty. She dropped the point of the knife into the cutting board and hung a wrist on the handle as she looked at me.

"Ah, I guess not. Sorry I asked," I covered.

"It's okay. I've had to ask that of myself," Betty said with slight head cock.

"I wouldn't."

I nodded.

"And you, you're not headed for New York and the big time?" asked Betty, "I expect there's some high-tone clients there that need their cards read."

Thinking of Wally, the tramp, I said grimly, "I don't eat out of trash cans. And I don't go to New York."

"Why not?"

"I've been there," I said, "there's nothing there."

CHAPTER 76

We ate our little meal, Betty eating her omelette and half of mine. She then dove into a heap of spaghetti and red sauce. She rolled careful balls on a fork and stuffed them in.

She talked between gulps. She could be marvelously funny.

At one point, I laughed so hard I caught a tear in the corner of my eye.

When the good cards turn up, I just let them come.

The Six of Earth, Beauty; The Earth Father; I recognized them.

I sat watching the beautiful Empress eating her pile of noodles.

CHAPTER 77

"The Water Mother is a card of enchantment and wonder at the riches of your inner world," I said.

After dinner, Betty had begged me to continue her reading. She had been surprised that I remembered her next card without notes.

She was sitting in Lotus position, cross-legged on my rug, a warm cup of tea in her lap. Her eyes were half-closed as I talked.

I'd shuffled her card out of a deck and laid it on the glass coffee table top, where it seemed to float before her.

"Your inner world is large and it reflects the world around you. The realm of water reacts to forces. Blue skies and calm seas, storms come and large waves rise. The Water Mother is the ruler of the waves and the beautiful blue seas. Like all seas, it is a realm rich with life. Life that rises and disappears. Life of astounding colors. Life with passionate open eyes for seeing."

"It makes me feel full," said Betty.

"That's the spaghetti," I said.

"So you are rich in your emotions, and the lesson of the Water Mother is to stay balanced. Within water is born the fire of the soul. In balance is fulfillment, to be, to love, and to express. Your emotions are a devine and holy realm, one which you should enter often and value."

Betty looked at me with a half-smile.

"You make it sound like a church," she said.

"Perhaps you can think of it as a church," I said.

"Do I get to keep the offerings?"

"Sure, write yourself a big check," I laughed.

"Feel deeply and you will know deeply. The feelings you cherish within will be the forces that flourish without."

"You are a person of deep feelings, through perhaps camouflaged by small waves of foolery and delight."

"I like the way you see me," said Betty.

"That's in the cards," I said.

"The Water Mother doesn't mean I'm going to have a baby, does it?" asked Betty with a bit of a grimace.

"No," I said.

"Thank God," said Betty, blinking her eyes at the ceiling.

"This card usually appears when you are at a portal, a period of transition. New things are about to arrive, and the Water Mother appears in guidance and welcome."

"Will there be somebody there to carry my bags?" asked Betty innocently.

I laughed, “No, it’s bring your own slave.”

“If you draw the Water Mother, you are often headed toward a new level of understanding. New forms are about to be created or adopted. The Water Mother appears to welcome you with love through the portal.”

“Nice,” said Betty.

“Yes, another good card for you.”

“Funny, I had a Chinese fortune cookie the other day that said the same thing. I opened it and it just said, ‘Big Things.’”

I laughed, “Well, I used to do readings of fortune cookies, but my clients got fat.”

Betty said, “That’s what you think my fortune cookie meant, Big Things: you’re going to get fat?”

“No,” I said, “I think it meant ‘Big Things.’”

“Meaning?”

I laughed, “I don’t know, I don’t read fortune cookies. It means whatever you took it into your heart as.”

“I can tell you what the Water Mother means, though.”

“What? Oops!”

Betty had jiggled her tea cup and spilled a blotch of tea in her crotch.

“The message of the Water Mother is: Take Joy, Go Forth.”

CHAPTER 78

Betty raised her wrist, looked at the black strap, and said, "I have to go." Her rehearsal was drawing near. I nodded. She thanked me for the reading and stood.

I said we could finish the reading another time.

"Your flowers, let's not forget those," I said. I walked her over to the bouquet, where Betty stood looking at them thoughtfully.

"They look too nice there," said Betty, "I can't take them."

"Do," I insisted.

"They'd look hopelessly out of place in my crumbling little apartment."

"Flowers are wherever you find them."

"No, they're yours. I can't. Besides, I'll get mine after the play. Leads always get bouquets of this and that from the stage ardent," insisted Betty.

I offered to walk Betty to the theatre school.

"Better than that, you can walk me home. I need to pick up my script before I go."

"You can come watch some of the rehearsal, too, if you like," said Betty. We agreed I had nothing better to do.

At my door, Betty said thanks for dinner.

"Of course," I said.

"And thanks for the Water Mother," said Betty shyly.

"Thanks for her, too," I said.

CHAPTER 79

It was an old building with a grey canvas awning sagging with age over the front door.

"This was the Hotel Jefferson until they condo-ized it," said Betty.

"I remember the Jefferson. It had a doorman with a frilly red courtier suit and black beret always standing outside. As I remember, he even carried a spear."

I looked at the old brick facade now blackened with traffic soot. Inner city tenement. I could imagine the scuffed wood floors and exhausted sofas inside.

"We're trying to get the landlord to bring back the spear. We have gang members who like to hang in the lobby."

Betty pulled open the door complete with duct-taped glass. As I stepped over the sill I was greeted with the smell of old rug.

"I live just up the stairs, no need for the elevator."

I looked at the battered wire cage just large enough for two to stand in. I was relieved I wasn't getting in. It looked like a quick ride to the basement.

Betty had romped up the two flights of stairs ahead of me. When I put my hand on the banister, it shimmied and creaked.

All dimness at the top of the stairs. The hallway was pond-water green. I realized the dark figure bending at a door down the hall was Betty. I waded in that direction.

When I stepped up to her, she said, "Just about got it." She'd been wriggling her key and pulling the doorknob in and out in critical adjustments.

"That's Andy's apartment behind you," said Betty.

I turned to see another door behind my shoulder. I noticed a front door mat on the floor that said, "No Way!" in big letters. Then I saw the mat was just a slab of cardboard.

"Have you lived here long?" I asked.

"About a year, it's close to the school and all." Betty straightened as the latch finally clacked back. She gave the door a shove and it swung back until it scudded to a stop on the floor two thirds open.

I was chewing my lips. I wondered what I was going to see.

Betty noticed. She laughed and took my elbow.

"Don't worry, I'll protect you," she said pulling me in.

Her hand still on my elbow, Betty's index finger poked an ivory button into the wall.

The lights came on. I blinked looking around. A great mooning chandelier with glass of pinks and blues lit up overhead. It was like the lights coming on for a three-ring circus. A flock of diamond prisms dangling below the chandelier broke the light into a swarm of multicolored fireflies flashing and winking on the walls. A variety of tall plants, palms, ficus, bamboos leaned like onlookers between well-framed posters of classic movies and Broadway plays. Despite a pair of pants on a chair and a pail yellow bra dangling off an end table, the room was clean and cared for.

I stood looking at the light. It dressed the walls with a leopard skin of rainbow spots.

"I took the apartment because of the chandelier," said Betty.

"It's almost alarming, it's...beautiful," I said.

"It's less so when I have on the other lights," said Betty. She pressed another switch. Around the walls an array of low light fixtures came on with the effect of stage floor lights. Betty walked across the room some twenty feet to a table and began rifling through paper stacks.

Betty's apartment was a large single room with one other door which I imagined led to a bathroom. A clean linoleum-topped counter and empty white sink stood against the far wall. A dresser and hulking armoire stood at attention against another.

And there in the middle stood a huge navy blue bed.

"That's quite a bed. It looks nearly the size of the Ark," I said.

"It's really old, Quaker country, but I bought it from a sale at the hotel here. The man said it was tremendously old."

"It looks sturdy. Maybe it came across on the Mayflower," I joked.

"No," Betty said, "The man said something about it being the Mayflower."

Betty sat down on it and made a couple of rump bounces.

"It's a hard old bed, but I like it."

"Sometimes I like to think about all the people that might have slept on it. Over the years in the hotel and elsewhere."

I shook my head.

"Not me," I said. I gave a theatrical shiver.

"Who knows, maybe your mother and father slept in this bed," challenged Betty.

"Please," I said, "Spare me."

Betty laughed.

"Well, I like it anyway," said Betty, rising after patting the bed as if it were a pet. "It has history."

"Will you take it with you when you go to New York?" I asked.

Betty shook her head.

"I really don't know."

Betty waved a sheaf of typed papers fastened with a brass fastener in one corner like an earring.

"I got the script, let's go, shall we?"

When Betty pressed the ivory button again, the room went completely dark.

CHAPTER 80

"Okay, let's get the props in place!" shouted Betty.

The auditorium was fairly large, nearly half-encircling a small stage.

Andy and two women in jeans and sweaters were sitting on the stage front with legs dangling. They began to get up as Betty called ahead to them with orders.

Betty stepped up on the low stage and centered herself among them.

I stopped silent a few feet behind her.

"Where's Clayton?" asked Betty.

The girls looked at each other.

Andy shrugged, "Late as usual."

Andy saw me standing behind, frowned briefly, then nodded with a grimace.

"I want to run act one tonight. From the beginning. Everyone have their script? We run this thing in two weeks, so you should know your lines."

Heads nodded.

"Who's that?" asked one of the girls. Her hair was red and fell down the side of her face in circling streamers. "Is he the New York guy people are talking about?"

"No," said Betty, "That's all rumor. It runs around here every play period. Get it? So."

“So who is he?” giggled one of the other girls. She had freckles and short blue hair in a crewcut. She wiped at her nose as she snickered.

“My name’s Jean,” I said, cornered as Betty strode off across the stage.

“Just a friend,” said Andy staunchly.

“Are you going to be doing Clayton’s part?” the blue-haired girl asked.

“He hasn’t quit, he’s just late,” said Andy sternly. The blue-haired girl cast a what’s-your-problem frown.

“Just a friend, here to watch,” I said.

“Okay guys, let’s get on with it,” called Betty loudly. “I need some help setting up here.”

Andy and the other girls turned from me and walked down stage. I stepped back several rows and took a seat.

The stage scenery consisted of a table, a dry bush, and a step ladder. A pitcher of water was put on the table. Betty kept referring to it as the fountain. The dry bush was a forest which was dragged as a hiding place center stage. The girl with red hair climbed to the top of the step ladder and I realized she was a damsel on a balcony.

“Okay, I want to get the pacing up a bit. I want faster speech. Smack it out. Fake it if you have to, but I want the audience listening hard, so that they get surprised by it and discover emotions,” Betty called.

Betty and the three other players readied in position.

"What about Clayton?" asked the red-haired girl from the top of the ladder.

"I'll read his parts," said Betty.

"Why doesn't he do it?" called the red-haired girl from the top of the ladder. She had a hand pistoled at my chest.

Betty looked my way with cocked-eye.

She held out the script, "Well?"

I shook my head.

The last thing I wanted to do was get up on stage and read lines.

Betty came down to the edge of the stage and looked down on me like an owl on its prey.

I cringed.

Betty pounced.

CHAPTER 81

"Okay, read toward Beatrice who is on the high balcony. Then to me," said Betty. She laughed at the face I was making.

I was holding the folded scripted awkwardly in front of me, squinting to read.

"Try not to scare your fellow actors," laughed Betty.

"I think I'm going to throw up," I said.

Andy laughed.

"This isn't me," I said.

"Come on just say it, no one cares," said Betty.

"Hurry up, this step ladder isn't comfy," called the red-haired girl impatiently.

I shrugged out an okay-here-goes. "She is a light in the window that breaks the pane of my heart," I read aloud.

"Louder!" shouted Andy, the two girls, and Betty almost in unison.

I looked around at each like a lighthouse casting light through the fog. "She is a light in the window that breaks the pane of my heart," I shouted.

"Good," shouted Betty.

The red-haired girl responded with her line from on high.

"Oh, you just make me want to pee my pants."

CHAPTER 82

It was a bad play. It took its content from simple role reversals, Shakespeare's play modernized, complete with lesbian overtones in which the blue-haired girl kissed the red-haired girl lingeringly. The emotions were forced, inauthentic, or exaggerated, leading too quickly to the contentious. I felt like I was speaking my lines with gravel in my mouth.

My young compatriots were in glory. As I stuttered uneasily, the young actors returned their lines with magnanimous fervor. Arms swept, heads bowed deeply. Comely eyes played my way. I realized that although I had a part, I was mainly an audience. Andy, a modern day fool and courtier, returned lines with stentorian confidence and shuffling hand movements posed theatrically. The red-haired girl let go a bawdy laugh that startled me and I stepped back. I could see she like that. Immediately she weaved in nearer like a snake at its prey and put her hand upon my chest. The script felt like a wagging fish in my hands.

"Keep it back, Michelle, you're the master's maid, not his whore," called Betty tonelessly.

I delivered three lines that were so foul I wouldn't have spoken them to a dog.

Andy nodded his head as if I'd given sage advice.

The play mainly centered on who would partner with whom. Everyone seemed a potential bedfellow for everyone else.

I seemed to be some passive hero.

At one point, Andy and I exchanged a short verbal dual over the red-haired girl. Meanwhile in the background, behind the bush, the blue-haired girl rubbed the red-haired girl's shoulders with her moaning in erotic ecstasy. Loudly. You would have thought a howler monkey had caught its tail in a tree.

Then Andy and I had some kind of chest pushing confrontation. I was unclear why we were play acting a fight.

Betty walked about as a trickster. Her role was to set up the plot so that different competing lover's oversaw each other philandering, calling for explosive fits of jealousy. Her name as Balthazrina. At one point, she climbed the ladder and pretended to be the red-haired girl musing to the moon about the blue-haired girl.

Andy's part took him into a cymbal clap of rage. He cursed the red-haired girl, his true love, and vowed to kill me, the hero. To win her back in a manly show of force. The reason he vowed to kill me was because the blue-haired girl couldn't reasonably be expected to lift a sword admirably. No red-haired adulation could be born of it said Andy dropping finger quotes. So he would kill his friend to gain the ambivalent lover.

The duel was on.

Andy and I squared off holding yard sticks on either side of the water-pitcher fountain. We jabbed and clicked sticks.

Andy leapt upon the table, taking my yard stick beneath his arm.

"I am killed!" he shouted.

Then he fell like a flour sack onto the floor.

"Well done!" said Betty walking up and clapping me on the back.

"Really?" I said with a sideways glance. Then I realized she was still saying her lines.

"Aye, you kabobbed him most royal," said Betty, hands on belt with a boastful laugh. "Let us hasten away!"

Arms overhead, Betty turned to the audience and shouted, "Curtain!" letting her hands drop slowly.

CHAPTER 83

A single pair of hands clapped laconically. Up in the middle rows, a large blond-haired youth lounged in the row with feet up, putting his hands together in ironic smacks.

"Excellent show, you really don't need me," called the young man.

Betty squared herself.

"You're late," she said.

The young man hoisted a shoulder and began ambling down the aisle.

"I see I've been replaced," he said. He was wearing a prim sweater and slim cut jeans.

"No, you haven't. You missed the first act," said Betty. She was holding her script against her leg like a pistol.

"If you're not going to be serious about this, it's going to be a mess," said Betty.

The young man bound up on the stage. He then stepped in close to touch or embrace Betty, who stepped back with stern demeanor.

"Yeah, I know," said the young man. I noticed his short blond hair was cut identically to Betty's.

"Clayton, let's rehearse, okay?" said Betty.

The young man shrugged.

"Anyone got a script?" he called to Andy and the girls behind.

I walked up and handed him mine, then I walked down off the stage and took a seat in a middle row.

"Thanks," called Clayton behind me with mild sarcasm.

"You were great."

CHAPTER 84

The second act was more of the same. It began with Betty standing alone in soliloquy revelling in having tricked the hero into killing Andy, who for no discernible reason was her sworn enemy. Betty went on about the foolishness of love and that life was cheating and people could even be cheated of life. The speech was elevated, flat, and baseless. No real wisdom purveyed. I could not even sum it as leaning toward any card I knew.

You can throw a deck in the air.

It's interesting to watch.

But it's not a reading.

Finally the young man named Clayton came on stage and wrapped his arm around Betty's waist, drawing her fast to him, as he leered and spoke of her tricks and betrayals. In theory, as Betty squirmed against him, he reviled her for having found her out. But as he spoke, his smile was not of revenge, but one of having captured prey.

Betty continued her lines bravely. She offered up the blue-haired girl as the real villainess who should be killed forthwith.

The play struggled on.

I left quietly.

CHAPTER 85

She was wan and drawn in the face. She said she'd never known love.

She came to my door just as the morning sun had touched it.

She sat with her shoulders hunched, solemn. Her head was a helmet of black lifeless hair, her face a bit bony and hollow.

She said she didn't believe love existed. She wanted to know if it did.

I nodded and shuffled. I always shuffle slowly when faced with great pain.

I threw two cards.

Five of Wind: Fear.

Six of Fire: Glory.

"Love exists," I said, "I've felt it."

"These cards mean, 'Give your love away, what the hell.'"

CHAPTER 86

He was old and he was bitter.

His grizzled chin and white hair made a halo around his head, his grim mouth, his squinted forehead.

His shirt was lank, with one pocket corner torn away slightly with loose threads. His hands scrubbed, his fingernails were white like teeth.

The card showed an abyss.

"I'm alone. My wife gone. My children, they don't like me."

"Why is this?" I asked. I sat with my thumb on the next card.

"When we were just starting out, I cheated on my wife. I saw another." He sneered at his hands. "Ever after that, it wasn't the same. I could never get the feeling back about my wife."

"My life soured. Marriage was endurance. I helped raise the kids, but I really wasn't interested. My wife, Lillian, she was young and open, and I watched it turn to ill-ease and distrust."

I sat silent.

"She never knew," said the old man hoisting his shoulders.

"But she knew," he said finally with a look as if he were holding a bitter penny in his mouth.

"Why did you hold onto this so long? You made this very important to you."

I turned over the card. It was The Star reversed.

"I persisted. I was a man."

I said, "You followed a false star."

CHAPTER 87

And that was that.

CHAPTER 88

At noon I locked up the shop and walked toward the Hotel Jefferson.

I stood for a moment out front, staring at its sagging awning and sooted face, feeling a complete fool.

I went in anyway.

The smell of the lobby was just as dank, the stairs and hallway just as dark.

I knocked on Betty's door.

I put my hands in my pockets uncomfortably. I heard rustling and a chair scrape from the other side of the door.

The door opened a pencil width with a slight chain rattle.

"It's me," I said.

After another moment of chain rattling, the door opened wide. Betty stood framed in it in white short-sleeved blouse and jeans. She was smiling, radiant.

"You came, all by yourself!"

"Yes," I said.

Betty's hand was on the doorknob, her mouth open. Her surprise and pleasure were deep.

"Well..." I said. I hesitated.

"Well, this must mean something!" laughed Betty.

"I guess. Can we figure it out inside?" I asked.

Betty laughed again.

"Come in. Come in!"

Betty ushered me in and closed the door. Then she threw her arms round my neck and kissed me.

"It's nice to be here," I said as she hung a moment against my chest.

"No kidding," said Betty.

CHAPTER 89

"You make me laugh," I said.

"I can see that," said Betty. She took down her arms and backed up smiling.

"I wanted to see you. Is it a good time for a visit?"

"Actually no. I have an exam in 30 minutes. Andy and I have an undergraduate final together. But I'm so glad you're here. Please, stay. Can I make you some peppermint tea?"

"Don't trouble."

"No, let me! I owe you some tea, and spaghetti!'

Betty turned hastily toward her counter and hot plate. As she sloshed water in a kettle, she laughed to herself.

"I can't believe you came."

CHAPTER 90

Betty brought over the hot tea, but before she set the cup down she kissed me.

I could feel her warm lips pushing my head back.

She took a seat opposite me at her table.

"I guess we're real friends now," she said.

"Safe guess," I said.

"I wasn't sure I'd see you again, after my play. You didn't like it, did you?"

"No," I said.

"You looked funny."

"I bet."

"You could be good if you put yourself into it," said Betty.

"I believe that was me in it," I said, "It wasn't good."

"No," laughed Betty.

"Andy was..." I shrugged.

"He was Andy. You can depend on big moves and a loud voice from him at least. The girls middling. Clayton, well," Betty shrugged unhappily.

"He's bad news," I said.

"I can handle him," said Betty, "He'll do as I say."

I nodded without understanding.

“Do you prefer old style Shakespeare? Was it too avant-garde?” asked Betty. “I mean you left before you saw the second act.”

“It wasn’t that,” I said. “I just wasn’t getting the why behind it. It was confusing.”

“You think life is all ordered and laid out and not confusing?” asked Betty amused.

“No,” I said.

“Well, what was it then?” asked Betty. “The story? Was it unbelievable?”

“Some stories are short, some long, some unbelievable,” I said. “It wasn’t that.’

I sipped peppermint tea.

“For me, it all just stayed on the surface. It never got down to turning over a card and just seeing what came up.”

In answer Betty raised her eyebrows.

“I’m not sure I need to do that, all I need to do is keep people entertained and thinking.”

Betty sat smiling at me, unconcerned about her play.

I shrugged and smiled back.

“Whenever I have mint tea now I’ll think of kisses,” I said.

CHAPTER 91

Someone pounded on Betty’s door three times and shouted. “Yo!”

"Be there in a second," shouted Betty, scooting out of her chair.

At the doorknob, she stopped and smiled at me before opening.

"Hey!" said Andy to Betty. He was all smiles. But the smile dropped as he saw me sitting at Betty's table.

Andy stiffened a bit.

"We going? We've got that test," he said.

"Yeah, Jean just dropped in. Is my anthology in your room? I can't find it."

"Oh, yeah, it's on the coffee table."

"I'll get it."

Betty jumped out of sight through the door, leaving Andy in the doorway looking at me.

I stood up and walked over.

"Nice to see you, especially after killing you in a duel," I said.

"You weren't too into it," said Andy.

"I'm not really an actor, in the way you are. I guess we don't share that in common."

Andy nodded his scruffy goatee without comment.

He looked over his shoulder at his open door across the hall.

"I guess not." There was the hint of animosity in his voice.

"We do have something in common," I said.

"Oh? What's that?" asked Andy, looking my way with a frown.

"You like her as much as I do," I said.

Andy looked at me. It was the moment of recognition just before rams butt heads. His eyes were clear and open. Finally he nodded.

"Except, I'm a brother and you're a candidate," muttered Andy to himself.

I had nothing to say to that.

CHAPTER 92

Andy, Betty, and I took a pleasant Spring walk to the theatre school. The sun was out, high and sharp, comforting on the back. People on bicycles rode by with short shadows.

The sidewalks were nearly white with heat.

Betty talked, asking Andy short questions about Renaissance plays, and occasionally stealing a glance at me that made me feel secretly included.

The air was sweet and fresh in the lungs.

"Andy, are you going to New York?" I asked.

"No, I'm going to class," said Andy.

"Not today, fool, for your career," laughed Betty. "He means are you going to stay in the kitty litter or move to Broadway, Bub."

"Broadway Bub will be my stage name," replied Andy dryly.

Betty giggled. I could see Andy knew how to make her laugh.

"Personally, I don't think New York is the center of the earth," I said.

"You don't?" said Andy and Betty in unison.

"Is everything a performance for you two?" I asked sceptically.

At one point, Betty stopped on the sidewalk to crack a book for some obscure fact that might be on the test. When we walked on, I realized that Andy was now carrying Betty's books for her. She rifled pages as she went.

"I always do my best studying on the sidewalk," said Betty.

"When does the cramming stop?" I asked.

"Twenty-third street," said Andy matter-of-factly.

Betty laughed. Then Andy snorted as well.

We finally came to the steps of the school where a milling whirl of young adults in circus costumes were cavorting. Some wore baggy pants and shirts in offending primary colors, others were in theatrically stitched rags and patches. A few wore red or yellow conical hats.

"Looks like Clowning 101," said Andy.

I spotted several older men standing to the side in clown suits smoking.

Betty caught my look.

"Some never graduate," she said.

CHAPTER 93

We reached the school steps and stopped.

"Can I see you later?" I asked.

Andy moved uncomfortably.

"The exam runs until 5:00. Then at 5:30 we're scheduled for the theatre to rehearse. You could come and watch again. Then we could go to Renaldi's for a drink or something," suggested Betty.

"I think I'll skip the rehearsal," I said.

"Don't be afraid, you won't have to do anything," laughed Betty.

Andy smirked and raised his shoulders waiting.

I shook my head.

"Well, just the drink then?" plied Betty.

I nodded okay.

"Well, if it isn't the case of 'Too Much Toad for Everything'," said a voice.

The blond-haired Clayton walked up and stood, chest to shoulder against Betty.

Betty turned on him as if pinched.

"Clayton," she said.

"Betty," said Clayton.

"Andy, here," said Andy to himself.

I laughed.

Clayton turned on me.

"And you must be Jean," said Clayton, snidely accenting the J.

"No, I'm just leaving," I said.

I turned to leave with a small hand wave at Betty.

Andy laughed.

"I'll come by for you after the rehearsal," called Betty.

I nodded.

"See ya," called Clayton in a mocking tone.

I left as the three young actors walked up the steps. Betty was framed on either side by Andy and Clayton, then she skipped ahead and disappeared through the door.

CHAPTER 94

When I opened my apartment door, there stood two harlequins.

It took me a few instants to focus from the plumed hats, ruffled collars, and puffy-shouldered bodices decorated in diamond patches to see the faces were Betty and Andy.

They were leaning in on each other's shoulders in a chummy pose.

"My two favorite fools," I said.

I stepped aside to let them come in.

Betty laughed and walked directly into the living room and flopped on the couch. Andy stepped in more tentatively, looking around as if for cobwebs.

"We came for you," called Betty.

"I see," I said.

"Betty told me about your place," said Andy. He'd stopped in front of the Gauguin with its heavy gilded frame and track lighting.

"How did the rehearsal go?" I asked.

Andy followed me into the living room.

"Better," said Betty.

"I suppose that's because I wasn't there," I said.

"Absolutely," said Andy.

Betty laughed.

"We managed to make it all the way through without a lot of bickering," said Betty.

"That's hopeful," I said. "And Clayton?"

"Oh, he did his lines," said Betty shrugging.

"Although he insisted on smoking the whole time, the ass," said Andy.

"He smoked during rehearsal? He needed a cigarette that bad?" I asked.

"He doesn't smoke," said Andy. "Pure pretension."

"Affectation," said Betty.

"However, he only coughed and spewed smoke once when I poked him during the duel," continued Andy.

I shook my head.

Andy had lost interest and was now walking quietly about the room looking at the day's flowers and bric-a-brac on tables and mantel. I noticed he was wearing tennis shoes under his tights and Elizabethan costume.

"So, let's go get a drink at Renaldi's. Work's over," cried Betty.

"You're going to a bar dressed like that?" I said.

"No, we have to pass by our apartments to change. The school would kill us if they saw the costumes worn out on the town."

"I think he meant he was ashamed to be with us," said Andy to a wall holding a small Asian oil.

"We don't hold your red shirt and boots against you," said Betty.

"No, not at all, I don't mind either of you," I said.

"Well said," replied Andy, "Pitiful, but direct."

"You know what I mean. All right, I pledge my undying adoration to you both," I said dramatically.

"Let's get out of here before this goes further," said Betty.

"Agreed," I said.

"Ditto," said Andy.

CHAPTER 95

Betty's and Andy's apartment doors had opened in opposite directions and the two costumed actors disappeared. I followed Betty into her doorway.

Betty had turned on her marvelous light. Sparkling rainbows hung in clouds.

"Close the door, will you?" called Betty as she pulled loose a string at the back of her neck.

I closed the door.

When I turned back, I found Betty shuffling off the top of her costume over her head, and then she was standing in tights with her bare back to me. I saw a beautiful S curve at the base of her spine. Betty quickly bent and wrestled her familiar purple sweater over her head and stretched it down to her waist.

"There we go," said Betty, turning with a smile.

"That was refreshing," I said.

I was advancing to kiss her when there was a knock on her door and Andy's voice rang out.

"Let's go!"

I opened the door. Andy stood in his shorts and yellow T-shirt. He had on black socks and black shoes.

"Formal attire?" I asked.

"Renaldi's won't let you in without shoes," said Betty.

"Or in sneakers," grimaced Andy.

"What about my boots?" I said. They were half-height, not quite cowboy boots. Just deep enough to hold the knife.

"You'll be a preferred customer," said Andy. "They prefer customers have shoes in case you need to kick the meatballs across the floor."

Betty laughed.

"Well, let's hasten away," I said.

CHAPTER 96

We walked several blocks through the general traffic and hubbub of a commercial quarter of boutiques, specialty shops, and small cafes. We passed an occasional corner liquor store, people in ski caps and flannel shirts standing with hands in pockets outside. We came to an area where corners were crowded with people waiting at traffic lights. Andy and Betty were in good spirits, pointing out the oddities of city denizens and dress. We passed packed shop windows showing imports, curios, and art in such a mass of crowding and creativity it seemed senseless.

A woman in short white dress and white boots, her hair scalped into a startling yellow crewcut, walked by leading a toy poodle dyed the color of bubblegum.

Andy stopped and watched the animal as it passed.

"I don't like animals that look like candy," he said.

"That doesn't make you much of a predator," said Betty.

"Renaldi's is two blocks that way," Betty reassured me.

We came to a street corner. On the sidewalk, amid waiting bystanders, a disheveled man knelt with his face and forehead on the cement. He was motionless, his knees drawn under him in fetal position. His light green clothes were dirty, black holes shown like sores on his shoe soles. Caked with dirt, his hands were beside his head out flat on the sidewalk. Beside him sat a small empty cardboard box.

As the light changed and the crowd walked around him unseeing, the prostrate man remained motionless, his face pressed to the ground.

"Funny, you always see that guy on a street corner, then in fifteen minutes, he's a little farther away, head down in a new place," said Betty, "But you never see him move."

"He circles," I said. "He's lost Mecca."

"Once, as a joke, I saw someone put a parking ticket on him," said Andy.

After two blocks, we came upon a shining cave with the sign "Renaldi's Taverno" above the door. Underneath the name was the subtext, "Eatsa Pizza!" College-age couples and three-somes where walking in and out. Door wide open, a bright hall was reverberating with crashing cymbals and disorganized electric guitar playing. Without hesitating Betty and Andy walked straight in. I followed a little doubtful a few paces behind.

The place was shoulder to shoulder with a laughing, drinking crowd. Round tables stood around the noisy room, each with its metropolis of bottles, glasses, and drinkers hunched under an umbrella of noise to hear each other talk. The band was stuffed in a far back corner where two or three feet of dance floor was packed with waggling girls.

Betty's hand shot into the air as she recognized and shouted hello to various patrons.

Andy and Betty hurried forward and took chairs at an occupied table. Their arms began wind-milling for me to follow. When I sat, I nodded to the two girls already at the table. Only on remarking one girl's blue hair did I recognize my fellow actors.

"Hey, it's our man from New York!" laughed the blue-haired girl.

"Hi," I said. "Not from New York, remember?"

"Hey, it's our man not from New York, remember?" said the blue-haired girl to the red-haired girl. Both laughed. I counted seven empty beer bottles and four glasses. They were drunk, but not drooling.

A waitress with hair that came straight out of her head as if it were electrified stopped for the order. Her eyes never looked at us as her vision swept around the room. Her pen seemed to tattoo our order on paper without her knowing about it.

I looked about seeing a menagerie of people of all sizes and shapes. Above the overly loud music was occasional laughter that went off like gunshots. It was a sea of unfamiliar bodies. Some people looked like dogs, some sleek cats, others like horses. People of every color and demeanor. There was no norm. It was all differences and most not so subtle. At such times, I realize I need the cards to see what's underneath and to make any sense of it.

"You look like you're sitting on the electric chair," said Betty.

"I'm not good in crowds," I said.

Andy's chin raised to a point across the room.

Betty's head turned.

"Clayton," she said. Her eyebrows arched a bit exasperated.

I looked to the far side of the bar where the young man Clayton was lounging at a table of four other cohorts. They were tilting beer bottles to their mouths and looking about the room dissatisfied. Clayton and his friends struck me as college hounds out for partying.

"He hasn't seen us," said Andy.

The red-haired girl elbowed her way up from the table. She tottered a bit, smiling, as she put her face down into Andy's. Andy recoiled the slightest, his goatee lifting.

"Let's dance," coaxed the red-haired girl.

Andy shook his head.

"Go on," said Betty. She offered a stern look.

Andy shrugged and got up. The red-haired girl led her catch in shorts and black shoes away. "Don't you think it's kind of fun to be here?" asked Betty, tweaking my ill-ease.

"Sure, similar to the zoo or a gladiator match," I said.

"To say nothing of cannibals," laughed Betty.

"Cannibals at least know why they're there," I said, smiling.

"Oh, I'd say this mainly has to do with mating, wouldn't you?" asked Betty.

"I hate to think about it," I said.

"Don't you think it's just a lovely, fantastic gene pool?" laughed Betty. Betty drew in a deep breath as if feeding on fresh air.

"When I go into the jungle I don't think of mating with everything in it," I said.

Betty laughed and the blue-haired girl blinked and smiled uncomprehending.

Our drinks arrived. The waitress set them down before us and left without looking.

Andy and the red-haired girl returned. Andy's face was one shade away from a grimace, but he was being a good sport.

He held the red-hair girl's chair as she fell into it.

Serious-faced, Andy had several drinks in a row. In between small talk and sight-seeing in the busy room, the blue and red-haired girls asked me questions about who I was, where I worked, how I'd met Betty. None of the answers seem to make sense to them. They merely blinked and asked the next question. On finding out that I was a card reader, the red-haired girl asked for her cards read.

"Sorry," I said.

"Why not?" asked the red-haired girl.

"He doesn't have his cards with him," said Betty.

"Some other time perhaps," I said.

The red-haired girl frowned, but then began hunting through the empty glasses for the remainder of her drink.

"Do you do card tricks, too?" asked the blue-haired girl.

I laughed.

"Do a card trick," insisted the blue-haired girl.

"He doesn't have his cards," said Andy distinctly.

Andy had another drink. He was getting wobbly now. Betty was laughing at him as he made jokes and did mocking quotations from Betty's play.

Andy asked Betty to dance and they went off to the dance floor.

I found myself alone with the slouching young actresses. They were both leaning on their elbows, smiling at me, but for no reason I could discern.

"Have you been in acting long?" I asked both faces.

"Forever," said the red-haired girl.

"Longer," said the blue-haired one.

"What roles do you like to play?" I asked.

"The girl who gets got," laughed the red-haired girl.

"Trés famous bitch," said the blue-haired girl. Both girls began laughing as they leaned against each other's shoulders.

Thankfully, I could see Andy and Betty making their way back across the room. Betty waved as she arrived.

"So we have the whole cast here," said a voice behind me.

I turned to find Clayton primly putting a cigarette between his lips as he looked down on our table. He was weaving just perceptibly.

Andy and Betty stopped at the table's edge.

"Clayton, what are you doing here?" asked Betty.

"Nice to see you, too," said Clayton.

"You said you were off with friends," said Betty.

"An obvious lie, no friends for sure," said Andy. Andy plopped into his chair and lounged back for comfort.

"I just dropped in with a few friends, over there," said Clayton, bucking his head in no particular direction.

"Well," said Betty. Then she abruptly sat down. She made it plain she was offering no invitations.

"Mind if I sit?" said Clayton to me.

Before I could answer, Clayton was at the table among us. He batted the ashes from his cigarette into a glass that just happened to be mine.

"So, Betty, do you think we'll be ready for the performance?" asked Clayton. His voice implied absolute unconcern.

"Some of us," smiled Betty.

"Not you," said Andy, dotting the i.

"Well, Andy, some people can think on their feet, others stink on their feet. How's the commercial coming anyway?" asked Clayton.

Andy did a heavy shrug.

"It's $600 bucks," he said.

"I wish there were commercials I could do," said the red-haired girl.

"Next time I hear a casting call for sluts I'll let you know," said Clayton.

"That's for me to know and you to pay for," riposted the red-haired girl unperturbed.

Andy laughed.

Clayton laughed as well.

"Children, let's try to get along. Be nice," said Betty.

"Or what?" asked Clayton.

"Or I'll jump across this table and claw your eyes out," said Betty. "And I mean it." She gave a carefree wave.

"What do you think of all this?" said Clayton turning to me.

"I certainly don't want my eyes clawed out by the beautiful senorita," I said.

"She'd be good at it, too," said Clayton.

"This calls for a sacrifice," chimed Andy, "Clayton, you volunteer."

"Pissant," said Clayton.

"Ouch, vocabulary, a most formidable weapon," said Andy.

"I think this play is doomed," I said.

Betty frowned.

"Oh no, just friendly bickering among the cast and other animals," said Clayton as if coming to the rescue.

"So it's always like this," I said with extreme scepticism.

"I guess that concerns us really, not you," said Clayton flatly.

"Unless you really are my understudy."

"I think not," I laughed.

CHAPTER 97

The blue and red-haired girls left to go to the bathroom. Clayton sat looking from one face to another.

"Betty says you're a card reader," said Clayton.

"Yes," I said.

"Bizarre," said Clayton.

His eyes raised from the table to focus on Betty.

"I'll know my lines, Betty, don't worry about it," he said, half in earnest.

"Good," said Betty.

"We'll make it through," he said.

Betty nodded.

Clayton was staring at Betty, twiddling his half-burned cigarette.

"Let's dance," he said to Betty.

Betty reared back just the slightest.

"No thanks," said Betty.

"Why not?" asked Clayton.

"Because she's pooped. She just danced with me," said Andy.

"Betty's the type of girl where no means yes," laughed Clayton.

"Then yes," said Betty. She laughed and remained motionless.

"Come on," insisted Clayton.

"I think it's completely clear," I interjected, "She means no means no, and yes means no."

Clayton turned and looked at me sternly.

CHAPTER 98

"So you're the type that horns in," said Clayton.

"I was under the impression that people were free to make choices. That slavery was over a hundred years ago," I said.

"I don't know," replied Clayton, stealing a glance at Betty, "I'll have to check next time I go down to the plantation."

"Good line, bad acting," said Andy.

Betty laughed.

Clayton drew in heavily on his cigarette. He sat weaving slightly as he stared his indignation at Andy. Andy was mimicking silent laughter at Betty. I sensed something was going to happen. Clayton turn to me. His eyes focused like a snake.

"So, Card Reader, can you read my future?"

"He doesn't have any cards with him," said Andy.

"I don't need them," I said, "I can read without them."

"Oh?" said Clayton, his interest perked. "What do the cards say about me?"

"Fear and pain," I said.

Clayton stiffened.

"You're predicting fear and pain for me?"

"It's not a prediction. Those are the facts," I said.

"Watch out for yourself," growled Clayton. Clayton half-rose.

"Them's the facts, Jack," laughed Andy.

"Clayton, maybe you should leave," said Betty quietly.

"Yeah, maybe," laughed Andy. The drink really had him.

Before I could speak, Clayton jerked Andy to his feet by the shirt front. He thrust the hand bearing the cigarette into

Andy's face, putting the hot tip a quarter-inch from Andy's eye. Andy froze for fear of blinding himself. As he blinked and winced, Clayton held him still with the burning cigarette poised at his eye.

"You are quite a card, Andy. Maybe you should be the one-eyed Jack."

A serious stillness fell between them.

Betty's eyes were wide, her mouth open.

I reached down into my boot. I took out my knife and poked the blade a quarter-inch into Clayton's thigh.

"Oww!" yelled Clayton. Releasing Andy, he jumped back wobbling and looked down at his leg where a red coin was blooming.

"You stabbed me!" shouted Clayton, looking up.

"It's the gypsy way," I said.

CHAPTER 99

By now there was quite a commotion around us. A waitress asked Clayton if she should call the police. Clayton touched his hand to his leg, then looked at his red palm. Wobbling, he looked hard at me. I was still holding the knife. His pride won out. He walked away to his friends at the far table to share his wound.

"We should go," I said.

Andy was furious, Betty shaken. I put down cash on the table and the three of us pushed through the crowd toward the door.

People divided around me as I led the way. I felt like I'd made a spectacle of myself like a man walking a high wire.

Finally we were outside. The three of us began walking home in silence.

CHAPTER 100

A high yellow moon leaned in the dark.

"Let's go sit in the park," I said.

I could see Andy walking with teeth gritted.

Betty's face was frowning, deeply shadowed.

As we walked onto the grass of the park, we could hear the high trill of frogs. A low mist hung in shallow pools across the delled ground. The sky was starry and clear, some stars gleaming like cat eyes.

We came to a wrought-iron bench.

The three of us sat. It was cold on the back.

"So," I said.

"I'm going to kill that motherfucking jerk," said Andy.

"Andy?" said Betty.

"Did you see what he did to me?"

"We saw," I said.

"It was so vicious," said Betty.

"I've posed problems for you," I said.

"What do you mean?" asked Betty.

"You only defended Andy."

"I don't need defending," said Andy.

"Don't worry, I stuck him because I wanted to," I said.

"I've threatened things for you."

"Threatened what?" asked Betty.

"Your play. And I've created an enemy for Andy."

"I take care of myself. You don't have to audition for the part," said Andy.

"I don't care about the play," said Betty.

"No," I said, "You have your future in it."

"Clayton's just an idiot. Don't worry about it," said Betty.

"Fuck Clayton, he's the problem," said Andy.

I could feel the foggy chill working up my legs. I stood up slowly.

"I didn't help either one of you," I said.

"Let's call it a night, let's go home," said Betty.

CHAPTER 101

We were halfway to Betty's apartment when she broke the silence with a curious question.

"Jean, why do you carry a knife?"

"People," I said.

Andy, who to that point had been sour and taciturn, laughed.

"You better get a bigger knife."

CHAPTER 102

We stopped in the hallway as both Andy and Betty wrestled with their doors. I waited hands in pockets. Betty got her's open first. She turned smiling.

Andy finally jimmied his open. He turned hesitantly as if expecting to see something he shouldn't.

"Night," he said.

"Jean, would you like to come in?" asked Betty.

Andy hesitated in his doorway.

"No, I think I'll call it a night," I said.

Betty nodded.

"Night all," I said and turned.

CHAPTER 103

On the way home I thought of Betty's play. My definition of sickness is when the whole tries to reject a part. It's a situation that leads to illness. And sometimes the patient dies.

And for myself, I remembered I had a Great Great Uncle who was well known for saying, "Well boys, we kilt us a whole lot of Indians today."

CHAPTER 104

People.

CHAPTER 105

The next morning was sunny and beautiful. I went to the shop. But there were no readings to do, so I decided to take a walk in the park.

Across the grassy grounds sprinklers were rolling, sending out spitting plumes of water that fell like arched wings to the thirsty grass. Mothers were pushing empty strollers slowly, kids toddling along side loose. Spring was already stepping away. The daffodils and tulips were on their last legs as some of the hardier summer flowers were venturing forth with reds and blues. I crossed the park headed for a little denser wooded area. It was a place of bright sunlight and cave-like shadows scattered among foliage. A place where a transient might camp down for the night or lovers come at midnight to steal a few minutes.

Among the thick fir trees was a hollow where a shaft of sunlight descended, hard as a spotlight, on the piney forest floor.

I sat on the bare ground in this circle of light.

I closed my eyes and reviewed lessons of the cards. Finally I felt better.

I opened my eyes when a squirrel began skittering through the trees overhead and dropping things.

I walked back through the park. You could hear distant traffic noises and the thin roar of airplanes high overhead.

As joggers in shorts criss-crossed the sidewalks left and right, I passed the sailing pond and caught sight of a little goldfish slowly meandering about.

I remembered my poet friend once told me you can't teach people to hum: it's an outlook on life.

I dropped over to McGregor's and ordered daisies.

CHAPTER 106

Betty was standing at my door in front of the shop.

"Well," I said, smiling.

"Hi," said Betty. Her head was tilted, her look a little sheepish, as she smiled at me as if squinting through bright sunlight. She nervously pushed up the sleeves of her purple sweater.

"I hope you haven't eaten. I owe you lunch," she said.

I felt a flush of happiness in my chest.

"Where are we going?" I asked.

"The only place I can afford," said Betty, "My place."

"Should we call ahead for reservations?" I asked.

Betty said, "No, I know the chef."

"And that would be you or me?" I asked.

"Me," said Betty.

"Then I guess I know the chef, too," I said, "And I'd recommend the place."

"Recommend it for what?" asked Betty.

"For everything," I said.

"You don't make any sense," laughed Betty.

"It's lunch. It doesn't have to," I said.

CHAPTER 107

Andy's door stayed shut as Betty rattled and struggled with hers. When she let me in, I saw her big blue bed, her window open on the Spring day. All was prepared: a small sunlit table pulled over by the window was dressed with silverware, clean plates, white napkins, and vase of two white roses. A fresh baguette had been sawed into coins on a plate. Two chairs faced each other across the table. Somewhere a radio was playing light rock music in low tones.

"Soup is on," said Betty, "I'll just heat it a bit, then course one."

"French onion," I said sniffing the air.

"Good nose. All in honor of Jean," said Betty.

"I suppose if I were John, it'd be peanut butter and jelly," I said.

"Yes, you eat according to the accidents of your birth name," said Betty.

"If I were Paco, I'd be having a taco," I said.

"I'm Betty and I like spaghetti," she laughed.

"And course two?" I asked.

"Lobster," said Betty. She lifted a kettle lid to expose a puff of steam and a large red homard. "And he didn't go quietly into that dark night."

"My goodness," I said.

"It's okay. It was an accident of his birth," said Betty.

I sat and spread a napkin in my lap as Betty leaned to ladle soup into my empty bowl. She put the soup pan back and then came and took her seat before me.

I sat smiling.

She laughed and clapped her hands, leaning forward as if she'd caught something fallen from the ceiling.

"Grace," she said.

CHAPTER 108

After several spoonfuls of soup, Betty said, "Last night you said my play was doomed. Did you mean it?"

"No," I said, "I was just being cynical and guessing. It seems like there's too much disruption lining up. With Clayton and Andy. And you and Clayton."

"I think in the end we'll make it," said Betty hesitantly. "I'm counting on their egos to be too big to screw up royally on stage."

"I suppose you could argue that," I said, unconvinced.

"It's just if they screw up, and blow my project, I may not get to go to New York for a while," grimaced Betty, "I want to get out of here."

"I don't believe people check for degrees on Broadway," I said.

"Maybe not, but I finish what I start," she said. "I may not be the most talented, but I finish things."

"Soup is good," I said, smiling.

"What if it's not in the cards for you to go?" I asked.

Betty reared back an inch. "Then I wouldn't believe in the cards," she said.

She hesitated.

"Why do people believe in the cards? I mean, why do they work? They seem to tell people about their future. Do you believe in them?"

"I guess it's a matter of degree. I believe in them more than that poor lobster does."

"Which ain't saying much," said Betty, "since he's boiled and all."

I laughed.

"Really, do they predict the future? Did my card reading say I wouldn't go to New York?"

"No, they didn't say that," I said. "They don't predict those kind of things."

"But one of your cards was The Mountain. That means it's a time of learning, work, and discipline. You are blossoming, it is a delicate time in your life. It's as if you were at the base of a Mountain, and if you walk one step at a time, though the slope is steep, you'll get there. You must be careful of false steps."

"I'm not too interested in climbing the mountain, I want to get to Broadway," said Betty.

"The Mountain is you," I said.

"And do you believe that's the truth for me?" asked Betty. Her forehead was slightly rippled.

I nodded.

"Do you like me?" asked Betty.

I nodded again.

"Then why don't you just make a big prediction for me? Say I'm going to be a big hit in the theatre?"

"You already are a big hit," I said.

She looked at me until she understood what I meant.

CHAPTER 109

"Well, we better have that lobster," Betty laughed.

"I predict he's cooked," I said.

Betty got up and went over to her steaming pot.

"Why do the cards seem to predict?" called Betty.

"Oh," I said, "Because they tell the truth. You can count on the truth. Like a prediction."

"How so?" asked Betty. She took a fork and gave the creature within the pot an experimental stab.

"Okay," I said. "It's like this: If I tell you the truth, it was true yesterday, it's true today, and it's very likely to be true tomorrow. So people take it as a prediction."

"I don't get it," said Betty looking up.

"Look, I draw a card. I say in the past your name was Betty. Today your name is Betty. And, barring catastrophe, you'll still be Betty tomorrow. It's a good prediction. I'm just telling the truth."

"So it's like saying, you have two legs, you had two legs yesterday, and tomorrow, you'll have two legs."

"Yes, as long as I tell the truth about what the cards say."

"And you're never wrong?" asked Betty looking over at me. She had the pot lid held like a shield at her waist.

I shrugged. "If I told a person she was capable of love, would I ever be wrong?" I asked.

"I suppose that wouldn't work on a dead lobster," said Betty.

"Never do readings for animals or the dead," I said. "They don't pay."

Betty laughed.

Betty took tongs and picked the big crustacean, red and dripping, out of the pot. She placed it steaming on a platter between us. She brought over two coffee cups and placed them in front of us. I discovered mine filled with drawn butter.

Betty produced two plier-like nutcrackers from her hip pocket.

"I predict a good meal," I said.

Betty laughed.

We dug in.

The shell was thick, but the meat good. Betty ran to the sink and brought back some lemon slices.

"I'm not sure how to start such a beast," said Betty.

"Let me help," I said, "I have an advanced degree in eating. I see it as a compliment to my fellow animals."

Betty and I munched and cracked hard shells. We talked and had a good time.

Occasionally Betty would look up with her mouth full, laugh and tilt her head trying to keep her food in. She was getting a bit giddy.

"I saw a friend of your's today," I said.

"Really? Who?" asked Betty.

"It was a gold fish in that sailing pond. He seemed quite the happy hermit," I said.

"Oh really?" said Betty, pleased. "He made it?"

I nodded.

"Well, now I'll have to go to the pet shop and buy him a mate," said Betty.

I put back my head and laughed.

"Mother Nature, she'll just never leave you alone."

CHAPTER 110

We finished up the lobster. The white inner meat had been good, especially shared with someone like Betty.

"Delicious. Thank you," I said.

"You're welcome."

"What's for desert?" I asked, smiling.

Betty got up, took my face in her hands, and kissed me.

"That," she said.

CHAPTER 111

"Get up," said Betty, taking my hand. As I got up, she stepped to the middle of the room. Betty crawled onto her ancient bed, where so many dreams were dreamt, generations of lovers lay, opened, and were known. Betty lounged back, pulling up her purple sweater to expose her bare chest and small breasts and opened her legs at the coat-hanger angle of invitation.

I didn't need to be invited twice.

I moved upon her, kissed her sternum and chest, then kissed her mouth until she was struggling and bucking to shuck down her pants.

I opened my own.

It was a lovely coital dance. She writhed, struggled, and rolled, working against me. She reached down and cupped my rear, hugged me, grimacing and arching, then gasped, and stilled a moment. She laughed.

I felt myself release within her. It was a lovely dance, one I was made for.

"I'm going to name my first child Rapture," I said, gulping for air.

She took my head in her hands, pulling my face to kiss my cheek, whispering, "And don't forget her little brother, Bliss."

CHAPTER 112

Betty and I dressed and went for a walk in the park. Betty wanted to see her goldfish. It was a pleasant walk. A high sky, sun on the back. When we got to the sailing pond there was no one in sight.

We looked into the obscuring water.

We only saw a faint blur of gold before it fish-wiggled away.

CHAPTER 113

"Why are you an actress?" I asked.

"Well, first I'm an entertainer, I'm out for applause. But it's more than that, underneath entertainment, you can weave a web of art."

"To do what?" I asked.

"Like you, to say the things that need to be said," said Betty.

"So you believe the world is worth saving?" I asked.

"It's worth keeping," said Betty. "Don't you think?"

"It's arguable. I don't see great reasons for sallying forth, lance in hand. The earth, life, it's larger than we are. You can hardly change it."

"You change everything you touch," replied Betty."

"Millions of years of evolution, literally the death of every living thing that isn't alive today, good deaths, most horrible deaths, these are the daily substance of life," I said, "You can let it be and it will take its course. You can work to change it and it will take its course still a thousand years from now. What difference what song you sing on stage now?"

"There are voices who sing out of the past who touch us today," said Betty.

"You mean the mournful songs of longing and separation?" I said.

"The songs of joy," said Betty. "You have sung it with me, haven't you?"

I blinked. "I think so," I laughed.

"It comes down to this: what is your life for?" said Betty. "If you live for just yourself, you never have to act. If you live for others, you must."

"Do you believe there are useless lives?" I asked. It was a thought that haunted me as I talked with many during my readings. The huddled, the bewildered, the paralyzed.

"Sure, most," said Betty. She said this with such calm, there was no denying her.

"Why do you do readings?" asked Betty.

"I've tried, I can't live without people," I said.

Betty pounced forward, kissing me, throwing her arms around my neck, then wrapping her legs around my waist as I tottered and tried to remain standing.

"I call this position The Monkey Tree," laughed Betty, drawing back.

"Why do I think I've been here before?" I said.

CHAPTER 114

Betty had a class to attend. I walked her back through the park and over to the theatre school. I dropped her off on the school steps.

She wanted me to wait, but I told her I would go to my shop.

After I left her, I was a half-block from the school when a young man in a red shirt stepped out from behind a parked car.

Clayton.

He positioned himself to block my path.

I stopped in front of him and looked at him.

"You got your knife today?" he asked.

"Always," I answered.

"Then I better get me one," said Clayton.

"I thought you only threatened people with cigarettes," I said.

"I ought to press charges and sue you," he said.

"Any judge and jury would mistakenly think I was a hero, protecting a friend. You know I wasn't. I was just having a good time stabbing you."

Clayton's face was hardening into the dull angles of ice.

"Let me give you some advice. Stay away from Betty. You don't know what's going on between her and me."

"Let me give you some advice," I said evenly, "Once you turn over a card, it's too late, you have to read it."

"Just do it," spat Clayton. He leered forward.

I waited to see if we would tangle.

"What are you so afraid of?" I asked.

Clayton opened his mouth so that I could see his lower teeth.

"Just keep out of it," he said.

Then he passed me, bumping my shoulder.

CHAPTER 115

I turned a card. Alone in my shop, I sat looking, thinking. I had gone earlier to McGregor's and bought several immense bouquets of flowers, trellis mixes of purples, yellows, oranges, blues. If I sniffed hard, I could easily bring their fragrance to mind.

I realized the flowers were not for Betty, though she might interpret them so.

They were for me. An ephemeral wall of beauty.

I sat thinking.

The card was Karma.

CHAPTER 116

Twilight, and the sunlight was lowering to the color of yellow wax when Betty came to my shop door. She came in and oohed and ahhed over the flowers.

She kissed me like she meant it.

She wanted to walk somewhere to watch the sunset.

We set out across the city walking toward Johnson Tower, an old building, yet the tallest in the city.

As we walked together, Betty chatted occasionally putting her hand on my arm or her cheek to my shoulder.

When we crossed the street at the tower, the evening traffic was thinning.

Stepping into an express elevator, we rose a dizzying 30 stories to the observation deck. When the elevator door opened, we stood wobbling a moment catching our equilibrium again.

We stepped out into the sky.

All around was a circular blue horizon, a background of fuzzy hills, a curve of ocean, and low city buildings dropped like a jumble of shoe boxes across the landscape. A few bridges stood out on water with necklaces of red glowing lights.

The sky was paling toward stars.

Betty took a long drawn-in breath.

"It's almost gone," said Betty, raising her chin at the sun, a flattening yolk on a blueplate.

"Nice," I said.

I walked uneasily to the tower's edge and looked down. It was as if the earth had completely fallen away. Yet, even here there were pigeons prospecting at our feet.

"Are you afraid of heights?" asked Betty.

"No," I said.

"You seem a little glum. Is it the sunset?" asked Betty.

"No," I said.

"Me?" she asked,

I laughed.

"No, you wish," I said.

"No, it's just my grandfather built this building. He was..." I shrugged.

"What?" asked Betty.

I looked at her.

"Ruthless."

Betty's eyebrows hitched.

"How so?"

"Oh, he was rich, he stayed rich, others paid. This building, it was a scheme to dominate the construction industry. He made a fortune in it."

"And you're not proud?'

"No."

"Why not? An edifice to his success. What could be wrong with that?"

"My father told me there were a lot of lives put into this building."

"I imagine it took a lot of people," concluded Betty.

"No," I said, "I mean lives. People in the cement. Union problems. When you realize it, it gives standing up here on this building a different feeling."

Betty nodded.

"It's a nice sunset anyway."

"Jean?" Betty turned squaring her shoulders to face me.

"Mmmm?"

"If I were to go to New York, would you go with me?"

"No."

Betty chewed her lower lip, then turned back to look out over the tower's edge.

"Why not?"

"Too many tall buildings," I said, smiling.

"It's the same sunset," countered Betty with a what's-the-problem hoist of her shoulders.

CHAPTER 117

Betty and I walked back to my apartment. We spent a happy evening cooking and talking. Whenever I sat, Betty would come and sit with her shoulder against me.

We laughed a good deal.

I made love to her on the rug as Betty struggled to pull me in.

We spent the night together in the dark, close in my bed.

CHAPTER 118

In the early morning, I walked Betty back to her apartment. The light was still gray with dawn.

Betty was quiet, the hair on the back of her head a bit mussed.

We were on the sidewalk still a block from the Jefferson.

Betty stopped.

"I'm going to New York," she said.

She meant it.

"I know," I said without looking at her.

CHAPTER 119

In the dark hallway, Betty working at her lock, the door behind her rattled, cracked open.

Betty and I turned to see Andy's face wedged in his door. As he saw me standing next to Betty in the early morning hours, you could see his wheels turning.

"Morning," he said glumly.

And he closed the door.

CHAPTER 120

"What is it that you want?" I said.

The old man sat blinking and confused. He'd come in, looked around, then sat down. He looked dazed.

He was working his mouth, but not saying anything.

"Do you need some water, old man?" I asked.

He nodded.

I went to the back of my shop and brought him a tall glass of water.

He drank half in one long pull. I offered a plate of cookies which he ignored.

I asked him some questions he couldn't answer. Although his forehead wrinkled, he just blinked and shook his head.

I called the police and told them I had an alzheimer's patient.

He couldn't say what he wanted, and he couldn't ask questions.

He was hoping the shop was home.

I threw a card while we waited.

Father of Fire.

He liked the horse.

"I was a cowboy. Laramie. I rode rodeo," said the old man smiling.

"I got throwed," he said.

CHAPTER 121

At 3:00 Betty and Andy showed up at my shop. Betty was lively and laughing, Andy less so with hand-drawn cat-whiskers painted on his upper lip.

Betty asked me along to walk Andy down to his commercial shoot. I closed up shop and we were off.

"How does your play look?" I asked Betty.

"You mean Clayton," broke in Andy.

"I guess," I said.

Andy grimaced. "He called me and apologized. Said he was drunk. What an ass, what an excuse for a blinding."

"What did you do?" I asked Andy, stealing a quick glance toward Betty.

"I have nothing riding on this play," said Andy. He flipped his hand to express his disdain, then continued, "But Betty does. So I just told the ass no problem."

"And rehearsals are on?" I asked.

"Yes, he's being real nice about it," said Andy.

Betty wouldn't look at me.

"I bet he even arrives on time tonight," said Andy.

We arrived at the building housing the BBEO advertising agency. A palm tree was planted in the lobby in a pool of shiny pink-marble floor tiles. A receptionist looked at Andy and simply pointed a finger at a far door down a hallway.

"See ya later," said Andy, departing.

Betty and I took seats on a yellow leather couch. I realized that this palm tree had probably never felt wind.

"Coconut?" asked Betty, as if offering a treat from the tree.

"I believe it's a date palm," I said.

"Well then, how about a date?" asked Betty.

"You're on. Thanks for asking. Where shall we go?" I laughed.

CHAPTER 122

"Glad to hear the play is still on," I said. We were walking to a small corner cafe that faced the river.

"Oh yes," said Betty. "We're almost to the end. A week and a half, two more rehearsals, and I'll be done with it." Betty blew out a tired breath.

"Then the new life," I said.

Betty looked over at me a long moment.

"I guess so," she said with a doubtful look.

We entered the cafe and took seats by the window. We watched a boat or two plod up and down the river.

I ordered coffee, Betty a creme brulé.

"Jean, won't you come to New York with me? Please? We could go together," said Betty.

"I don't think so," I said.

"Why not? Why not?" said Betty accusingly.

"What would I be, a card reader to the glitteratti?"

"You'd be with me."

I looked on with a pained smile.

"What you want is there in the future. What I want is here with me now."

"She's not here for long," warned Betty.

CHAPTER 123

Betty and I sat together in the cafe as the evening fell. The blue walls of night were descending all around.

"Tell me why," said Betty.

I shook my head.

"I've lived alone a long time. It's what I know how to do."

"You'll fuck me on a rug, but you won't get on a subway with me?" she said.

"Please, Betty," I said. "It was wonderful. Don't take it back."

I felt cornered. Betty leaned back in her chair and tilted her head.

"The trouble with you is you don't like people."

It was true. I looked at myself and saw that like a doctor who mainly sees diseased and sick I had a jaded view of people, the troubled, the twisted, the seeking who came to me as a card reader. I did individual card readings because I didn't like people as a whole. Betty looked at my face seeing me struggling with this.

"I think that's true," I admitted. I had to draw in air about that one.

"And if you don't like people, how can you perform your art for them? You don't have an audience."

I felt the weight of years of isolation on my shoulders, palpable and heavy. And this meant I had chosen solitary confinement.

"People who come to me, they want me to help them, tell them the thing that will make them feel better. Provide a scrap of hope, no matter how false. I, I have trouble respecting that. Even you, you came to me for a reading, looking for something."

Betty shook her head smiling. "I'd walked by your shop several times."

"I didn't come for a reading. I came in to meet you."

I felt the sun turn on somewhere inside me.

CHAPTER 124

Over the next several days, Betty and I traded off serving dinner in each others apartment. Wherever we ate we spent the night.

Andy had dinner with us in Betty's apartment one night. He'd been festive and jovial, talking of the directing foibles during the production of his commercial. He said they'd done a close up of his smiling face as he squatted in cat costume in a litter box. Betty grabbed her sides and laughed until she nearly fell from the chair as Andy demonstrated his grimaced smiling.

"And best of all, no pebbles in your bed!" said Andy, making an O with his finger and thumb next to his cheek.

Betty shrieked, a tear squeezing from her eye.

Andy performed proudly. I laughed.

Betty begged for mercy.

CHAPTER 125

When Betty picked up the phone and said hello, her face sobered. I sat on her blue bed watching. Andy had gone home. Betty stood silent listening into the receiver.

"All I want from you is to be at the rehearsal and do your part. And I want you to do it right in the performance. So be there. You owe me."

She put down the phone. She stood a few seconds looking at it sternly.

She looked at me.

"Clayton."

She wouldn't speak about what he wanted.

CHAPTER 126

Betty went to her window and looked out on the darkening city. She stood with her hands on the window sill, her back arched. City lights were showing through the park trees in Christmas tree pinpricks. The sidewalks were dark, no strollers, as a few cars nosed their headlights down the street. A distant siren spread its banchee call a mile away.

"I often stand here, looking out my window, just wondering about it all. Sometimes I pretend I'm in New York, you know, just to see how it feels."

"And how does it feel?" I asked.

"Oh," sighed Betty, "The same."

She turned in and looked at me. She had a strange smile on.

"The window is a symbol of the Emperor. He is the guardian of the kingdom. The window is the frame through which you see out, and through which you see in. If your Emperor is large enough and kind enough, he will let in the future."

"Of course," said Betty.

"Then we better just draw this shade," she said. "We don't want any Emperors seeing this."

Betty pulled down the shade until it nearly touched the floor.

She shucked off her pants. She turned around wearing only her baggy purple sweater.

I undressed as Betty turned off the lights except for her beautiful chandelier.

Betty and I lay together on her blue bed, looking at her marvelous light. A fantasy of diamonds and multi-color blossoms netted the walls.

Betty threw her cool thigh over my midriff and was atop me. Upright, pulling me into her, she began grinding her hips against me, eyes closed, her skin and breasts rainbow spotted.

She worked, bumping and leaning. I wasn't sure whether it was the old bed squeaking or Betty.

When we finished, she snuggled down under my shoulder. She was breathing hard. Her bare chest was damp against mine.

"Hope you enjoyed that," she whispered.

"Mmmmm," I said.

Yet I knew this was somehow a performance. It wasn't real.

CHAPTER 127

"Jean, one thing's for sure. Once I'm finished here, with the play and all, I'm not going back home. I'm not."

Betty had said this suddenly out of the dark.

I squeezed her to comfort her worry.

CHAPTER 128

The next day in my shop, I saw a number of regulars. In between readings I thought about this girl who wasn't going home and who wasn't staying here. She had a story to write and she wanted me to be part of it. But it wasn't my story. And I don't tell stories.

I read cards.

CHAPTER 129

It was the night of the final rehearsal. Betty was worried that there was a week lay off between the dress rehearsal and the performance. She foresaw rust on her actors, especially Clayton who was still recalcitrant and stumbling on certain lines.

"We just have to get through it," she said.

I had fixed her a heavy dinner of pasta in my apartment, but Betty had been nervous and eaten only a little cottage cheese and a canned pear.

"At least Andy and Clayton aren't fighting," she said. "Andy is being standoffish, and holding back, so the fight scene is very stilted, but he's giving Clayton room so they don't go eyeball to eyeball when Clayton misses a line."

"It'll work," I said, smiling.

Betty laughed.

"You are so unconvincing." She balanced her fork in my direction accusingly.

"Sorry, bad acting," I said. "But don't worry. I'm sure something interesting will happen up there on that stage."

"That's what I'm worried about," said Betty with a grimace.

"I think it's amazing Clayton is still in it," I said.

"Yes, well he is," said Betty with a half-hearted shrugged.

"Why do you think that is?" I asked.

"Me," said Betty.

"Have you been clear enough about your relationship?" I asked.

"Oh, yes," said Betty, "Very clear."

"And he's still supporting you. That's something," I said.

"He's not supporting me. And he's never supporting me! He supports himself," Betty said. Her forehead had wrinkled and she'd said this with real anger.

"Sorry," I said.

"No, it's not your fault. Let's just forget it," said Betty looking down into her plate.

"I just have one more rehearsal, then the play, then that's it," she said.

"Right," I said.

CHAPTER 130

I sat high in a back row watching them set up. Betty had asked me along for support. I'd said this might complicate things with Clayton.

"He can get over it," said Betty flatly.

Betty was in a pink Elizabethan fluted collar, red embroidered jacket, and black tights. Her blond hair was covered by a red Peter-pan hat with wagging pheasant feather. She waved a sheaf of papers and stomped from place to place across stage as she showed others their final marks.

The girls in long gowns, pink and blue, one with a high dunce cap draped in a veil, the other in a white hat that sat on her head like a flower pot, stood as a nodding choir. The red-haired girl's breasts were nearly popping out of her bodice. Andy was in black shirt and puffy pants that made him look like he was wearing an inner tube, except for a yard stick sword slipped in a huge leather belt.

Clayton was dressed in a navy-blue velvet cape which flashed orange whenever he lifted an arm. Which was often as he gestured and spoke, overly grand.

The table and water pitcher, the naked ladder, the dry bushes were in place.

"All right, let's do it! Can you hear me okay, Jean?" called Betty.

I nodded.

The final rehearsal got underway. Players took their positions without a lot of hesitating. Lines began, the actors moved, it was an ordered march.

I watched the first half-hour as the players vulgarly wooed, tricked, and cheated each other. There was a good deal of loose passion, mainly directed toward the girl with the popping breasts.

Andy, however, seemed to keep some distance from Clayton. When he delivered lines, he leaned back with a slight indignation. If Clayton hesitated, or needed a prompt, Andy leaned forward, hand on sword. Toward the end of the scene Clayton kept turning more and more to Betty for help. Andy began tapping his toe.

Clayton put on a walk so cavalier his cape swayed.

The play moved on. Things seemed to be going okay. Betty nodded, and only occasionally pointed out a new mark or shouted a cue.

"Louder!" shouted Betty.

Finally the red-hair girl was kissing the blue-haired girl passionately behind the bush, and Andy and Clayton began the duel.

Both started at each other with enthusiastic chops. Yard sticks flexed and clicked. Then Clayton lunged.

The tip of his yard stick poked Andy in the chest. Andy's face winced and his hand moved to his sternum to catch the pain. Clayton laughed.

I could see Andy's anger. And holding his chest, Andy looked over at Betty, sternly, then he slowly laid down and died.

"Aye, you kabobbed him most royal," shouted Betty. "Let us hasten away!"

"Curtain!"

Miraculously, the curtain closed as if on its own, and then in a few brief moments opened again.

Betty stood center stage for her soliloquy.

"My Lord, what fucking fools men be," shouted Betty to the back row.

CHAPTER 131

Her speech was one of gloating at those she had tricked.

"One thinks that cheating is a way of life, and that the art becomes the artist. But in truth it is nature's most abundant resource that becomes both my paint and canvas for my treachery! Ignorance, that resource, is so laughingly free, and yet so cherished and held dear that it sets them upon each other's necks. Ignorance that sees diamonds in a stone and for which one would kill one's own brother, that abandons child for yet another woman's snatch, that makes us puppets saying our father's words when our fathers were even more ignorant, and hence our betters! Aye, Ignorance, you make of men the king of dunces. And where you make one cry Love, you make another cry Foul, and yet each would know you in all your orifices."

Betty threw back her head and bellowed, "Dear Ignorance, you are the substance of the past and the propulsion of the future! For with you, our loves, our lives, our dreams, our goals, our disasters, our hatred, our vengeance, we see not the difference. A women's tit or a star's repose, we know it not."

Betty laughed, preparing to bellow again.

I sighed deeply.

"Ignorance you love us deeply!"

The curtain slowly closed. Betty made a sweeping bow with doft hat.

CHAPTER 132

When the curtain reopened, Andy was standing shouldered between the two girls. They clasped hands and bowed.

"One two three four, and up," shouted Betty. Then the caped Clayton came forward and bowed from the waist. Last Betty, arms out in crucifix, walked out for her bow. Clayton gestured to her, then step forward, putting his arm around her shoulder.

They bowed together. As they came up, Clayton squeezed her to his side. Betty bent and pulled away.

"It's my bow," she said and walked off. Clayton raised a hand and shouted, "Betty!"

Betty trotted up the aisle to me. It seemed she was hurrying to get away from the stage.

"What did you think?"

"Mmmm," I said.

Betty laughed.

"You hated it."

"Was that Shakespeare?" I asked.

"No, just some stuff I put down," said Betty, "How was it?"

"Dreadful," I said.

Betty laughed again.

She swiftly turned her back from me to the stage.

"Okay, be here an hour ahead of time the night of the performance. That's five days away, so practice your lines. Let's get the props stored. Thanks all," Betty shouted.

CHAPTER 133

That evening Betty came over to my apartment. I fixed a meal, but Betty seemed tired and distracted. She ate little, though putting a good face on it, and complimenting the food as if it were a pet sitting before her.

I watched with an even eye. I figured it was the prospect of the play finally coming that held her.

I asked if she would like me to do a reading, but she declined.

"I don't really want to know," she said with a nervous grimace.

"We usually don't get a choice, it just a matter of when," I said.

"I always hoped that ignorance was bliss," said Betty.

"I'd guess the ignorant would say it ain't."

Betty shrugged and smiled.

I took her out for a midnight walk in the park. I hoped the darkness and night air would free her.

We walked hand in hand as the moon rose, a thin harvest sickle.

We came to a large bush of lilacs. Although it was dark you could still smell the evening release of fragrance. I went to pull Betty into me to kiss her, but she stepped back.

"What's wrong?" I asked.

"I'm just out of sorts," said Betty.

"Is there something wrong between us?" I asked.

"No," said Betty.

I stood silent.

"It's other things, things you're not a part of," said Betty.

"Like the play?" I asked.

"Yes, the play and other things," said Betty.

"Sounds mysterious," I said.

"It's probably nothing," said Betty. She took my hand and pulled me toward the park exit.

"When you want to tell me you will," I said.

CHAPTER 134

I went home to my own apartment. Betty had asked me to drop her off, she needed some time alone.

CHAPTER 135

The next morning I went to my shop and opened it. Betty had said she'd come by in the afternoon. I bought new flowers and waited.

At noon a fat man came in with a troubled face. I could tell it would be a long hard reading.

"I need some advice," he said, his forehead sweating.

"Does this have to do with fears?" I asked.

"No, it doesn't," insisted the fat man. He looked at me reproachfully, his cheeks rising.

I knew now it did and it would be a arduous reading.

"Swallow your fears and you gain weight," I said.

He didn't like that.

I placed ten cards face up on the table. I knew there would be certain ones he wouldn't be able to look at.

CHAPTER 136

At three o'clock, I looked up to find Betty pushing through the door unsmiling.

"Hi," I said, getting up.

"Hi, Jean," said Betty.

She came forward and gave me an energy-less hug. She then sat down at my reading table.

I took a seat across from her.

"Sorry about last night," she started, "I just needed some time alone. I was kind of worried about something."

"It's okay," I said. "Can I help? Is it about your play?"

Betty shook her head. Then I saw her chin was quivering. She looked up at me with a pained and pleading look.

"I'm pregnant."

I sat silent.

"I didn't want to find out until I was late. I took one of those tests this morning."

"Me?"

"No, Clayton. Weeks ago, he told me the condom he'd used may have rolled down, released some sperm."

"You didn't do something? Get some contraceptive foam or a night-after pill?"

"No. He told me a week later."

I sat still taking this in.

Betty grimaced, "It was kind of a confession."

"I'm sorry," I said. Betty looked at me, her eyes filling, then she looked away. She pretended to itch the side of her nose.

"So," I said. I looked around.

"So," said Betty. She shrugged without resolution.

"Does Clayton know?" I asked.

"He doesn't know for sure," said Betty.

"But he told you a few weeks ago? About the time you broke up with him, right?"

"Yes," said Betty.

"And he's still in your play because he thinks you may be..."

"I told him he had to be in the play, he didn't have a choice," said Betty.

"Why is that?" I asked.

"Because he didn't give me a choice," said Betty. Her anger rose into a blush on her cheeks.

"I see," I said.

"I just came in to say I'm sorry. I didn't mean this to happen, I'll understand if you hate me."

"Hate you? Hating you is not in the cards," I said.

Betty winched as if pinched. "Please, Jean, don't be kind to me, it makes it harder."

"All I feel is kindness for you," I said.

"Please, Jean, don't. You don't know what you just said," blurted Betty. She put her hand to her forehead as if to catch a sudden pain there.

"I just want you to forgive me, so I can go. I have a play to put on, and I don't want the whole world angry and disappointed with me."

She was doing her best to hold it in.

"There's nothing to forgive. It just is. The whole world doesn't care."

Betty looked at me. "I'm sorry, Jean."

"Don't feel bad about it. We'll figure it out."

"No," said Betty firmly. "I'm doing this myself."

CHAPTER 137

Betty and I had lunch together. We went to a small cafe a few blocks away to have sandwiches. A stately calico cat with arched tail and silken coat met us at the door, brushing against Betty's ankle.

Betty and I took chairs outside eating in the sun.

She was taking small morose bites. She nodded as I made small talk.

"Betty," I said, "Do you want me to marry you?"

Betty looked down in her lap. She refused to look up.

She shook her head no.

"That's even less right than my black-mailing Clayton into the play," she said.

"Maybe not, maybe it's a good thing," I said.

"I have a play to do. And I want to go to New York," insisted Betty.

"I'm not setting up house and having a baby any more than I'm going home to live with my religious father. Oh, this is all so humiliating."

"I understand. I don't know if I can help you. But I understand," I said.

"Jean, I have to go think about things. Do you mind if I go home?"

"Go," I said, "I'll get the check."

Betty looked at me and pain flooded her face. Her hands began searching through her pockets, coming out with a twisted five-dollar bill.

"No, I have to pay. You can't always be paying," said Betty, smoothing the bill next to her plate.

Then she ran from the table.

CHAPTER 138

I needed to think about this. It meant that I couldn't open up my life just a little bit to slip in Betty. It meant I had to open it up to let in Clayton, too. He was a part of this. As Andy was a part. As the red-haired and blue-haired girls were a part. It meant I couldn't exclude from my line of view. In my readings, I was like a doctor, letting in a closed clientele, one that needed my services. What was beyond the door was beyond the door. I couldn't read cards for them all.

But now, with Betty's entrance, I also had to let in the world. She brought it in with her. I had to let in the people, the hordes I saw on Ricki Lake, Jenny Jones, Jerry Springer. The dundering, the ignoramuses, the feeders in the slop-buckets of ignorance.

My little card reading shop was like a tunnel through which no one could reach my clean-carpeted, lily-white apartment.

And now that Betty had entered my home all that had changed. It was like a blast had shattered a great hole in the wall, and there was a view of the park, flowers, and the city.

I was stunned.

CHAPTER 139

That evening I had a call from Betty. She asked me not to come over.

"Maybe it's better if we don't see each other for a while," she said.

Then she hung up.

CHAPTER 140

Several days later, I still had not seen her. I'd called each day receiving an excuse. Now was the morning of her play, and all I could do was call to wish her luck.

She hesitated and said thank you.

"Will you be there?" asked Betty.

"I don't know, should I?" I asked. There was a long pause.

"I don't know, it's up to you," she said.

"Okay," I said.

"Well, bye."

"Bye."

CHAPTER 141

At three that afternoon, Betty came to my shop. She entered with a hesitant half-smile, then came and sat down at my black tabletop.

"Hi," she said.

"Hi, shall I draw a card?" I asked smiling.

"No, I came to give you this," said Betty. She shoved a flimsy pink rectangle toward me the size of a business card.

"I hope you'll come," said Betty.

"Can I come early and help you set up?" I asked.

"No, no, I just wanted to make sure you would be in the audience," said Betty.

"I am in your audience," I said.

Betty smiled. As she got up to leave I wanted her to kiss me, but she went out the door without turning back. The card on the table was the Five of Earth: the Nadir.

CHAPTER 142

The inner theatre was in a relaxed hubbub. The grey curtain was drawn tight. An outlandishly dressed assortment of theatre students stood in small huddles up near the stage. I saw frizzy topknots, handkerchiefs around necks, broad belts, red boots, a single embroidered glove, and what had to be a false tattoo that descended from one girl's eye like a spiderweb. Heads were thrown back, laughter thrown out like lariats. I saw large gestures of pleasure and pain as they laughed and grabbed their stomachs or foreheads as if shot by arrows. In the middle rows sat the more sedate and proper. These were mostly perusing programs. In the back rows middle-aged professors and academic gentry sat stiffly waiting in suit-coats and turtle necks like a well-dressed jury.

I descended the aisle, pink ticket in hand. I was surprised to see only a few vacant seats in ones and twos scattered across the auditorium. My seat number took me down front to the second row aisle. I was center stage among the laughing thespians.

I felt uneasy. The brouhaha continued for several minutes, then the lights dimmed. There was a quickening of pace, people speeding up their last remarks before departing for their seats.

A high wheezing music with flutes, stringed instruments, and drums began a waltzing Elizabethan bump.

Late comers were wading to their seats down the crowded rows bobbing like ships on rough seas.

"Ladies and Gentlemen, 'Too Much To Do About Everything,' by Beatrice Jolliette."

I recognized Andy's microphoned voice.

The theatre lights waned and the hall went black.

The curtain pulled back to reveal a well-lit Spartan stage with only the few meager props.

Clayton strode in with a flash of orange and blue, raising his arm, shouting to someone off stage. Andy stepped into view after him.

"Aye, these women will be the death of me. There's the rub," complained Clayton.

"Aye, and rub them you will. Every one of them, my Lord," said Andy churlishly.

The audience laughed and Clayton bowed his head in acknowledgment just a notch.

Andy and Clayton began an exchange of lines that seemed to be going well. The audience laughed again. Then the two girls came on in their pink and blue gowns. They walked so closely together they appeared joined at the shoulder. They moved as one person, and you could tell one of the girls, the blue-haired one, was intimidated. She kept looking around uneasily.

Betty paced onto stage and stopped with her arms crossed.

The actors began regaling each other with loud voices and large gestures. The pace was fast and the audience strained to hear.

Then Clayton forgot his first line. His face went blank as he stared off stage.

Andy stepped forward and said Clayton's line as if thinking aloud. Clayton lurched alive and began his part again.

Betty walked about the stage urging on the others and making catty asides. The play moved at a pace so brisk there was no time for the audience to react.

Then Clayton forgot several more lines, each time with Andy looking on sternly and stepping forward to fill in. The two girls remained huddled together as if for warmth.

Betty and Andy bickered in a clearly well-rehearsed fashion, taunting each other with such finesse that the audience clapped.

Turning unexpectedly, Clayton bumped Andy who stepped back into the dry bushes and jumped as the twiggy branches stuck his rear.

The audience laughed.

The plot lifted off as the different couples began to woo each other and Betty wheedled as go-between for each. Plots were hatched, snares set. Andy's and Clayton's rivalry grew. The audience was carefully following the story.

Then the play began to fall apart. Clayton forgot more lines, looking more and more baffled, licking his lips. At one point, the blue-haired girl kicked the table with a painful thud and danced on one toe. Clayton squelched a laugh at his fellow actor's pain.

"Aye, me thinks something is afoot," he shouted, looking out at the audience for approval and receiving laughter. Andy stared his disapproval.

The dialog continued as lover's drew closer.

The red-haired girl climbed the ladder for the balcony scene, then began surreptitiously wiping her nose. Soon all could see her cheek and upper lip were a gash of red. Her hands were a red mess and spots were dripping down her blue gown. Finally, she gave up, climbing down the ladder and dashing off stage, her hand under her nose.

Clayton's head turned nearly around like an owl's.

Betty and Andy came forward with ad-libs, trying to fill in the blanks. The blue-haired girl's voice was so faint that not even the other actors could hear her. She went early and took her position alone behind the dry bush, crouching as if to stay out of sight.

Chairs began creaking in the audience.

Clayton was caught completely off guard. With noone to woo on the ladder, with no cues coming his way, he began sucking his lips and stuttering, trying to think what to say.

Then Clayton's cape fell off and people in the front row tittered.

Andy came forward and single-handed tried to recite missing parts. He directed his hands about to show the dazed Clayton where to move. Andy continued feeding Clayton lines, which Clayton tried to return, but with a stilted delivery.

People in the audience were coughing. There was a gentle murmur beginning near the stage.

Betty was standing stiffly to the side.

Andy came forward, loud and rancorous, trying his best to carry the scene. He backed Clayton into position for their duel. Andy was now reciting his and Clayton's lines at a furious pace. He seemed nearly mad, speaking to himself. From time to time, Andy would stop, waiting for Clayton to respond. But each time, Clayton failed to do more than open and close his empty mouth, wide-eyed like a landed fish.

Finally it was time for both men to draw their yardsticks and fight.

"En Garde," shouted Andy.

Clayton merely stood and blinked.

"En Garde!" shouted Andy, louder, waving his stick under Clayton's nose.

Clayton frowned, saying "What is this shit? Say your lines right!"

Andy's anger broke. He came forward and pushed Clayton on the chest.

Surprised, Clayton toppled backward, knocking over the table and water pitcher on his way down. Broken glass and water slew across stage with Clayton landing seat first in it.

The audience gasped.

Clayton bound up. His teeth gritted, he charged Andy grabbing him by the shirt front.

Both actors spun, wobbled, hit the ladder which slowly tipped then fell on the floor with a great slam.

Andy tumbled to his back dragging Clayton down on top of him. Both were raising elbows struggling to punch.

As the two entangled actors cursed and rolled, the curtain shut. It seemed to take forever to close. Yet banging, furniture screeches, and scuffling continued.

"Stop it! Stop it!" was shouted. It was Betty's voice.

A silence fell that left the audience nervous.

We sat for moments bewildered in the dark.

Then the curtain drew back. There stood Betty, her back to the audience, looking apprehensively off stage, her hat crushed in her hands.

Ashen, Betty turned blinking toward us. You could see her catch a breath as she discovered all eyes on her.

CHAPTER 143

The silence was a wall. Betty looked hastily around like an animal seeking to escape. She raised an arm above her head as if something were falling on her.

"Oh, this mess," she gasped.

She half-turned on the uneasy crowd.

She looked into the audience, squinting out.

"Oh, what have I done? This mess I created. Look at it! All ugliness and stumbling. Oh, God. I've done this. Oh, it's me!"

Betty's lips were shivering. She gulped.

"I've hurt you," she said looking blindly into the audience for someone. I realized it was me.

"And now this disaster I've created, this stage of clowns. Me in the middle. Why? Oh, God. I've damaged love. I've ruined it." She was blinking back tears.

Betty wobbled on stage. She sat down, then put up a hand to shield her eyes from the bright light.

"It's horrible." She shook her head.

"I didn't mean to. But look at me in all this ugliness, me in the center! I have hurt you. And here I did everything to please myself. You'll never want me now. You won't want to even know me. How did I do this? It's all falling to pieces. All a big shambles. A big god damned mess."

Betty put down her head and wept.

It was The Tower.

She looked up in my direction through the dark.

"Oh, it's too much. I've ruined it."

She shook her head.

"So here I am." She sat looking out into the black audience and silence.

I went up and knelt by the stage.

"I'm so sorry. I didn't see. I didn't see what I was doing in front of you all," said Betty, sweeping an arm around at the audience. "Now, look at me. A big god damn farce. A sickening person."

All eyes held her.

"Making sickening acts on a stage. When I should have been performing acts of love, real acts of love, instead of staging things for myself."

Betty fell forward burying her face in her arm.

The audience stirred uneasily.

I stepped up on the stage.

I went and picked her up.

I walked her into the wings. Off curtain, I put her down, and she clung to my chest. With her ruffled collar, she buried her face against me, shivering and weeping. I held her in her in defeat. And then behind us, I heard screaming, yelling, tremendous applause.

CHAPTER 144

The next afternoon I walked over to Betty's. The Spring sun was out, playing with shadows in the trees, the school children skipping home with the feeling of Summer coming. Great lilac bushes were purple bursts.

I walked remembering Betty's quick flight from the theatre, her refusal to go out for her bow. None of the actors had. And yet the applause had lasted for nearly a minute to the empty curtain. Each actor bore his or her own chagrin. They didn't care to carry it out on stage again.

There'd been no cast party or after show drinks. All had left in their own directions.

I'd walked Betty home, but she'd had little to say, except that she'd clung to me briefly before she entered her apartment door and locked it.

I called through the closed door that I'd come back tomorrow to see her.

With morning come, the Jefferson Hotel stood stony and resolute. I went in.

I climbed the dank stairs into the murky hall.

I knocked on Betty's door. I rapped several times then gave up.

I heard Andy's door rattling and his face appeared looking out.

"Andy, have you seen Betty?" I asked.

Andy looked at me, “She went home. She said to tell you she was going home for a while.”

“Will she be back soon?” I asked.

“I don’t know,” Andy shrugged.

“Was she okay?”

“I wouldn’t say she was overly happy about the performance. Man, what a disaster. Bizarre, but everyone who’s talked to me thought it was the best play on earth,” Andy blinked, “Man, if they only knew. Even the profs are discussing it in the halls. Friends are calling me Andy the Madman. Can you imagine?”

“You were really out there,” I said.

We laughed.

“Yeah, I was out there.”

“You were out there. And you knew why. It was a good performance,” I said.

Andy nodded, he gave me a half-smile from his scruffy goatee.

“Hope she comes back soon.”

“Me, too.”

I walked home alone.

CHAPTER 145

Over the next several days I walked to Betty's each morning and again in the afternoon. My knocking on her door was hollow and unreturned.

I walked back to my shop. I found I was not much interested in reading the cards, other people's or mine.

I felt returning the same universe of separation between me and others that I had grown up with, that Betty had eased a bit. My father, unrelenting in his drive to accumulate, had accumulated me as a kid, and I had gone unseen. He'd wanted me to share in his accumulations, but I'd been uninterested, so there was no core of shared interests. You can only say "Wow, what a neat car, wow, what a big building" so many times. Thereafter was silence. Which inferred lack of appreciation.

My father had once said to me as a kid, "You could find a million dollar bill in the street and you wouldn't be happy."

He was right. What good was finding a piece of paper that everyone else wanted and that wasn't mine?

"You'd walk right past," he said. He'd looked at me with his hawk-eye and hooked nose, a moment of irreparable, irrevocable judgement.

And in return, I saw—a damned pirate. Who kept my mother in jewels in a back room and who would rather she didn't vote. I had a nanny who took me to the park. Need I say more?

And one day my Mother slipped me her tarot deck.

It was in a black cloth bag and she said never to lose it.

"You have to learn your real foundations," she said. And then she smiled.

Funny, a single kind gesture can start a career.

CHAPTER 146

"What is this card again?" he asked. His forehead was wrinkled and he was confused.

With irritation I said again, "The Hanged Man. It marks a period of ill-ease, waiting, recovery."

"I don't get it," he said, shaking his head.

"Think of the frozen ground before Spring. The suspended animation of a space traveller unconsciously drilling through space."

"No," he said.

"Think of Sleeping Beauty reclining in her glass coffin, uncaring of the many dwarf loves pining around her."

He shrugged.

"Think thick ice," I insisted, "Water building behind the dam. The rotting log. The stuck elevator. The circling airliner holding in a landing pattern. Waiting for test results. An ambulance ride. The minute before the toaster pops."

I looked at him as he only sat blinking.

"A warning of an approaching hurricane. Grumbling about what you should have said, or rehearsing what you're going to say."

"The portion of your favorite song that you can't remember the words to."

"The urge to howl at the untouchable moon."

"Why did I have to get this card?" he asked.

"Because we don't have a dunce card," I thought.

I shrugged in return.

"You just do."

I sighed. He was so deeply buried I couldn't shuffle him out of it.

CHAPTER 147

That evening, as I came to the Jefferson, I saw the taillights of a cab pull away. I entered the dark lobby and hurried up the stairs.

In a heavy coat, Betty was leaning toward her door. Beside her was a large bulky suitcase. She was frowning as she unsuccessfully tried to thread her key into her lock. Finally she gave the door an exhausted push, then turned to pick up her suitcase.

"Betty," I said.

When she looked up, her face was haggard with deep pockets under her eyes.

She looked briefly at me fiddling with her keys in her hand, then looked down.

"Jean," she said.

"Let me get that," I said, advancing. I pushed open her door and Betty walked slowly through. I picked up her suitcase. I was surprised to find it picked up easily, it must have been nearly empty.

"I'm glad you're back," I said. "I've been thinking about you."

"I went home," said Betty.

Betty took off her coat and it fell lifeless across a chair then slipped to the floor. She went over to her large bed and sat. She looked down at her hands between her legs. She didn't seem to have anything to say.

"Are you all right?" I asked.

"Oh, yes," said Betty. She didn't look up.

"Everything is taken care of."

"What is?" I asked.

"I went home. I told my Father. He called a doctor he knew. That's all," said Betty. "Jean, I'm really tired. Can I just sleep?"

"Sure," I said.

Betty lay down on her side, her hands cradled between her knees.

She closed her eyes.

I sat down on the bed beside her. I pulled a blanket over her.

I sat with my hand on her shoulder until I was sure she was asleep.

CHAPTER 148

Betty stayed in bed over the next several days. She was deeply depressed. I stayed with her in her apartment, making light meals that went mostly uneaten. We conversed, but on light topics. Her voice remained low and her hair unbrushed. Each day, I went out and brought in a great vase of extravagantly arranged flowers.

"Please, you're going to make everyone think somebody died," said Betty. Then she caught her breath. Her face crisped with pain.

She returned to bed.

Andy popped in several times, but each time, his spirits sank and he became solemn as Betty barely responded to him.

One day I coaxed her into taking a walk with me in the park. I pulled her purple sweater over her shoulders and smoothed out her hair with a brush. Betty gave me a half-smile.

Hand in hand, we walked out of the Jefferson and across the park lawns. I sensed Betty taking in the fresh air.

We walked in a long cement curve to the little sailing pond. There, basking in the sunlight, a fat little golden blob floated, moving his fishy tail in infinitely small squiggles, bobbing and sucking unseen particles from the shiny water surface.

"Oh, he's still here," said Betty. She smiled briefly.

We watched the fish intently feeding off the water.

We had a good walk.

Later, on the way home, Betty stopped on the sidewalk.

"I have to go talk to Clayton," she said, frowning.

"Do you mind?" she asked me.

"No, of course not," I said. "You must."

CHAPTER 149

That evening I was cooking dinner. I turned, spoon in hand, and called, "Spaghetti for Betty."

I saw the white teeth of a short smile.

During dinner Andy came over and sat down to eat with us. Betty seemed glad to see him. Andy explained that Betty had received an A for her class project. Betty only shook her head.

"What a gift," she laughed.

Later that evening, the three of us played scrabble. The evening ended with us putting down the jumbled letters of imaginary words, laughing, released from the rules, making up definitions.

Late that night Betty kissed me lightly.

"Jean, would you mind sleeping in your own apartment?" she asked quietly.

"Sure," I said.

CHAPTER 150

Over the next several days, I called on Betty in the afternoon. It was hard for me to wait till then, but I felt I had to.

Each afternoon, she looked stronger and more beautiful. Her short blond hair stuck up in a stiff crown as she opened the door smiling.

I kissed her and she accepted it for a moment before she pulled back.

"I called Clayton," said Betty. She smiled uneasily.

"What did he say?" I asked.

"He wondered why I hadn't called sooner," said Betty, shrugging.

"I went to see him."

I nodded.

"He said he was sorry he forgot his lines," she said.

"He was happy to see me."

Betty looked like she was holding a bug in her mouth that she didn't want to swallow.

"What did you say then? Did you tell him about going home?"

Betty shrugged.

“I told him.”

“What did he say?” I asked.

Betty shook her head looking at her feet. She picked up her wrist in the handcuff of her own fingers.

“He cried,” she said.

CHAPTER 151

Several days later, I knocked on Betty’s door for our daily visit, but there was no answer. I noticed Andy’s door ajar, so I poked my head in.

“Hey!” Andy called putting down a mop he was wrestling against the floor.

“Is Betty around?”

“I heard her door close. I think she went out.”

Andy brightened.

“Hey, I had some good news. They want to go national with those cat commercials I was in. They want me to do four more, they’re paying $12,000 bucks.”

“Wow,” I said. Then I added gruffly, “That’s g-r-r-reat.”

Andy laughed. I noticed a scratch on Andy’s forehead that stood out like a red caterpillar.

“What happened there?” I asked, gesturing to his brow.

Andy’s mouth pulled aside comically.

"Clayton came by. He wanted to know if I was the one who told Betty to go home for an abortion."

"And he hit you?" I said.

Andy ducked his head and laughed.

"Well, that's okay, I kinda hit him first."

CHAPTER 152

I heard a violin squeal and looked up at my door. I'd been sitting at my table idly turning cards the entire day.

Clayton stood in the doorway. He looked sour.

"Hey, Fortune Teller."

His sarcasm was pretty thick.

He was standing halfway in the door with one hand on the knob, the other pushed under his jacket in a Napoleon pose.

"I'm a card reader, not a fortune teller," I said.

"Well, what card is this?" said Clayton.

He withdrew his hand from his coat to hold up a gun, showing me its rectangular L.

Seeing he still had his hand on the door knob and wasn't striding to the table edge to shoot me, I knew he was just waving it.

"It's called 'Idiot with a Gun,'" I said.

"Can I ask you a question?" he sneered.

"No, let me finish," I said, "It's actually 'Just One More Idiot With a Gun.' I've seen a lot of this card. Gun held by a hollow man. Another fucking self-centered actor. Ah, yes. You're the reason I don't want to be part of the human race."

"Shut up and answer this," said Clayton. He waved the gun vaguely in my direction.

"Did you tell Betty to go home and get rid of the baby?"

"People pay me to answer their questions," I said. "No matter how stupid."

"I'll pay you with this if you don't answer me."

"You have no intention of using that gun," I said. I pulled out my knife and held it up.

"But I have every intention of stabbing you with this," I said. Clayton turned the gun a little more in my direction in case I jumped across the table.

"Why are you so afraid? You brought a gun, you must be afraid of something. Most people ask questions without guns."

"Maybe I'm looking for the person who screwed things up for me."

"You're just looking for a reason, when it's just you who fucked up. Bad actor and bad faith."

"The audience loved me in that play," said Clayton, raising chin in riposte.

"It wasn't good until it meant something. You weren't even on stage then. You forgot your lines, then you had nothing to say, when all you had to do was say anything."

"At least I'm doing something. I would have taken care of her, if she hadn't met you."

"So you offered her a little part in the play 'Let's Have My Baby'?"

"I would have done the right thing."

"And you're surprised and afraid because she didn't want the part?"

"We could have done it."

"Your arrogance is astounding. You're afraid you can't live up to your own high opinion of yourself. You're afraid to do anything right," I said. "A hundred years from now I'm sure we'll all remember your name."

"Ten years from now, you'll still be sitting there flipping cards," said Clayton.

"Get out," I said.

He sneered at me and then backed out the door.

CHAPTER 153

I looked down at my knife. I didn't realize I hated people so deeply.

CHAPTER 154

When I get strong reactions, I know I'm close to the truth. Close to the person's real character. The character hidden underneath that fifteen minute's worth of polite sociability, the facade people carry with them everywhere. Under the social masks we wear at the grocery store and post office. Under the costumes, hairdos, and gestures of our defenses.

And my goal in readings was a frustrated wish that the client would go underneath, see the truth, and learn.

And here I was, having a strong reaction to Clayton.

What was it about him that was stirring up my truths? What was it about him that I was reacting to?

His arrogance, his aloof self-centeredness, his conviction of his own superiority founded on a thirsting need for approval?

Was I arrogant—and hiding it?

Was I aloof and self-centered—and hiding it?

Was I convinced of my own superiority and thirsting for approval?

I realized it was those very characteristics in Clayton that made him so useless to me.

I looked at my knife in my hand.

Perhaps I was just as useless to others—and hiding it.

CHAPTER 155

Betty was standing at her sink, washing up her dishes after our lunch, when suddenly she bowed her head. She stood vibrating with her shoulder's hunched.

I realized she was crying.

I went and put my arm around her.

"What's up?" I asked.

"Oh," started Betty pulling tears from her cheek, "I never imagined that I would go home and do that. I didn't intend to make decisions like that."

"It's bothering you?"

Betty's mouth pulled aside with a what-do-you-think grimace.

"Did you want to keep the baby?" I asked.

Betty shook her head.

"It wasn't really a baby yet. At that stage it's just multiplying cells, just like all my cells are splitting and multiplying all the time. I produce those cells every month. There's nothing unusual with losing that. It's just that this one had a potential of its own. And, well, I decided against it."

"I think it was the right decision," I said.

Betty nodded.

"But it was ugly. The worst. And to have to ask my father for help. That, well it was humiliating."

Betty went over and sat on her blue bed with her hands between her knees.

"Did he say things to you? Did he want you to keep it?"

"Sure he did," Betty admitted. "Oddly, that's a reason I didn't."

"How so?"

Betty took a deep breath.

"Oh, he talked to me about responsibility and sins. You have to take responsibility for your sins. We're all sinners. We have to accept the punishments that come. I should keep the baby, and accept it, and go on. God's plan and all. You can't know where it leads."

"Sorry, did he bully you? I don't know your father," I said.

"No. He was all kind and calm and soft spoken, the way he always is. It sounds convincing at the time."

"But…," I said.

"Why would you bring a new life into the world as punishment for your sins? Why would you doom a baby to be a punishment? Where's the love in that? When I want to have a baby, it'll be at the right time for the right reasons. So it will have its own potential, not just a future as my mistake or punishment."

"And you're okay with that now? I asked softly.

Betty shook her head.

"No, but that's my punishment."

CHAPTER 156

"Jean, what are we doing together?"

We were walking the park. It was warm enough that there were umbrellas up on the grassy meadows, families in flower-colored shirts bedded down everywhere.

"Walking home through the park?" I said.

"You're hopeless," Betty said, "You know what I mean."

"Do we have to look ahead?"

"Don't you want to know where you're going?"

"I'm walking with you," I said.

"Today," said Betty.

"Today is good."

"But, don't you want to be with me tomorrow?"

"Oh, this hurts," I said playfully.

"Come on, Jean, I don't get it. Are we together? I don't want to make another mistake and be with someone who secretly doesn't support me. Has me for his own reasons. I want us to be together, do things together."

"Including go with you to New York," I said.

"Yes, if that's what we decide. What's so wrong with that?"

I looked about at the park I knew, the city I grew up in, where I knew my place and felt safe from its dangers.

"There's something about New York that turns my stomach," I said. "I think of the mass of people I don't know, their crudity, false desires, false dreams, hidden pretension to violence. I just see nothing there. Nothing there for me. Not my childhood, not friends, not ambitious goals to be attained. It's just an emptiness that is so, so disappointing," I said. "Sure, I could go there, but I'd still be alone there with you."

"You don't know all that about New York," said Betty.

"I know all that about what's inside of people, the majority of them."

"How does that affect us and being together?"

"I doubt that I can give my caring to more than you," I said. "The rest, I don't care about. I have nothing to give them."

"And so New York represents an uncaring world to you."

"Well, I definitely don't want to live there."

"Not even if I go, wouldn't you want to go with me?"

"Is that what I do, follow another through a world like that? What happens when people project back to me my uncaring, my disdain. It will never work for me."

"That all seems pretty complicated, Jean. And I have to say, a little fearful. It sounds to me you'd be surrounded by your own pain."

I nodded. But I knew that was a lie: this wasn't just pain.

"Perhaps you should choose a different vision," said Betty, "Maybe you should be more like me."

"Perhaps you could give lessons," I said.

"Sure, I can make you my shadow," said Betty.

"That's the problem," I said.

"Okay, truce, I'll just take you the way you are for now."

"Minus New York?" I said.

"Minus New York," said Betty.

CHAPTER 157

New York would never be for me. There never was a Land of Oz. The Land of Oz was just a fanciful projection by a writer. You have to watch out for the projections you live within.

Some thinkers say your actions are the sum total of who you are.

But our actions spring from our projections, things that we have within us, that we bring into the world. Betty's play was a projection of herself. In my card readings, I projected meanings from the cards onto other people. They accepted those meanings and they reacted or acted differently. It was not just my actions, my turning over the cards, it was my projections of my inner truths that I put out there that affected people.

Projections represent a transition of spirit from the inner world into actions in the outer world.

And then, the world projects back.

The reaction to your inner world always comes back. You project smiles, you're likely to receive smiles. You project hostility, you'll likely receive it in return.

Betty saw me surrounded by my uncaring, my isolation, and my pain.

But I wasn't concerned about that.

It was my rage.

Clayton could get drunk and threaten Andy with a cigarette. But it was me who pulled a knife and stabbed. At the right circumstances, the right insult, I was ready to stab in earnest. My anger with the disappointments of other people's conduct was huge. I knew that in my arrogance I was relatively lawless, that with the right threat toward me or another, I could do great harm. Worse, I knew, like my Father, I would be good at it.

I had discovered a rage that was out of proportion. I suppose it was the pent up feelings come from my isolated contacts with people. And even though I suppressed it, I still kept a knife in my boot.

And that rage, it had really nowhere to go. Did I really want to just transport it to New York? Walk around like a ticking bomb? Chase someone down the street because they delivered the wrong pizza?

CHAPTER 158

He should have been incredibly bitter. Several years in prison. Three divorces. Bald, rolly polly, 50ish. Yet he was unstoppably jovial. He had a business that was shaky, but plans for another. Banks were threatening foreclosure.

I'd thrown some tough cards, but it appeared he'd get through.

He didn't seem worried.

"It would seem to me that you'd be incredibly angry," I said.

"I had to learn what to do with anger," he said affably.

"Which is?" I asked.

"Less rules, more satisfaction," he said. Then he laughed and patted his belly like some kind of buddha.

CHAPTER 159

Over the next several weeks, Betty and I took small outings to parks, beach, and now the Museum of Modern Art. We'd strolled the glassy hallways and galleries looking at a miscellany of huge paintings hung like windows. The old ones seem overly refined and out of touch, the new ones used vibrant colors which seemed younger and emotionally appealing.

"I had a call from Clayton today," said Betty off-handedly.

"Oh?" I said.

"He wanted to tell me he's leaving for L.A."

"Should we call L.A. and warn them?"

Betty gave me a cheerful grimace.

"That's not the best part," she said.

"What?" I asked.

"He's joining a boy band," said Betty.

"He's musical?" I said incredulously.

"He's going to sing and play the bongos," said Betty.

"Wait long enough," I said, "And all foes vanquish themselves."

CHAPTER 160

"What is it?" I said. I'd come over to check on Betty, but when she opened her door, she squinted at me uncertainly and nodded.

"Hi," she said.

"How you're doing?" I said.

"Okay. Thanks, Jean," said Betty. Then she came forward and put her head on my chest. I squeezed her.

"Something came in the mail today," she said.

"Oh?"

"It changes things," said Betty.

"What was it?"

"Here. You better read it."

Betty went over to the table by the window and picked up a letter. She put it in my hands and then backed up and sat down on her bed. She held her hands between her knees waiting.

"Who's Longine Productions?" I asked glancing at the letterhead.

"New York," said Betty.

I read:

Dear Ms. Jolliette,

It was my pleasure to recently attend your debut of "Too Much To Do About Everything" at St. Gerard School of Theatre. I must say, I enjoyed the play and especially your performance. Your soliloquy was powerful and transformative. I want to congratulate you on a fine job.

I also want to invite you to an up-coming casting call. We're reviving an adaptation of St. Joan of Arc and to date have found no one capable of the lead role. I would very much like you to come and read for us here in New York. We've made all the necessary arrangements to fly you out and for your accommodations. Readings take place at the WhiteLight Hall, Tuesday 7:30 to 9:00 and Wednesday 1:00 to 3:00.

Please have your agent or representative contact Jane Mitchel, my co-producer and director at 202 555-7723 to confirm arrangements.

Congratulations again on a fine performance and I hope to see you in the near future.

Sincerely,

Robert N Nausbuam

Producer, Longine Productions

I looked up.

"I think you're going to New York."

I found Betty looking at her window.

"You are going, aren't you?" I asked.

Betty nodded to the window pane.

"Yes, I'm going."

"Funny how things work out," she said lifelessly.

"It's what you wanted, it's come, now it's time to go," I said.

"It's strange though, that when you finally get what you want, it's not the thing you want anymore. Don't you think that's strange?"

"Yes," I said, "That's so. But you should take it anyway. It's here."

Betty shook her head.

"No, because, now, you see, I don't want to go there without you."

"Betty," I said, shaking my head.

"That's okay, Jean, I understand. You don't want to be my shadow. You don't have to. I'm just saying what I want. Is it because you don't want me?"

I shook my head no. I didn't have an answer.

"They're just people," said Betty. "You can screw up fantastically in front of them and by tomorrow they've forgotten your name. They don't care really."

"There's nothing there for me," I said.

"Nothing?"

I put my arms around her.

"You go. This is for you."

"Yes," said Betty. "Will you go with me to the airport at least? I leave tomorrow morning early."

Betty picked up a ticket from her bed that I hadn't noticed before.

She waved it like a windshield wiper briefly. Then she put her hand to her face crying.

"Oh, Jean, I didn't want it like this," gulped Betty.

I sat beside her and put my arm on her shoulder.

"It's okay," I said.

CHAPTER 161

That evening as I came up Betty's stairs, I saw the hallway filled with colored lights. Andy's door was open and loud music, electric guitar and drums that sounded like ricochetting thunder were beating out from his door.

I looked in like a man peeking in on a gunfight.

"Jean! Come in! We're having dinner at Andy's!"

Betty stood up. She was dressed in a light yellow short-sleeve blouse and white skirt. As she waved to me with bare arm, I saw she had a lanky golden watch on her wrist. A small glittering party tiara crowned her head with red and blue rhinestones that made her look like a superhero. She stepped forward to take my elbow.

Andy had a shiny green cone on his head. He raised a spatula from his kitchen counter where he was wrestling with something in a bowl.

"Crepes! Incredible crepes!" he called.

"Andy's giving me a party. Isn't that nice?"

"We're having Crepes Beatrice," shouted Andy. "They're filled chock-full with ham, cheese, and hot sauce."

"Sounds delish," I shouted.

"You better say that," laughed Betty.

"I'm going to be a star," called Andy dramatically. He raised a spoon to his forehead, then headed to attack a skillet on his hot plate.

Betty ran two arms under my shoulders and hugged me.

"Let's dance," she said.

We danced a minute or two in slow steps even though the music was crashing rock.

"Mmmm, this is nice," said Betty to my neck.

"It's only for a couple of days, you'll come back."

Betty stepped back. She made a half-smile. "Sure," she said.

"Launch number one," yelled Andy. "Straight to the great ship Broadway!"

As Betty turned down the music, Andy held up something golden, lank, and fried on a plate.

"Crepe Beatrice for everyone!" he called.

Smiling, Betty took me by the hand and led me to Andy's table.

"So, what do you think, Betty's heading for New York. Isn't that great? Life happened just like it's supposed to," said Andy.

"It's not certain, it's just a casting call," laughed Betty.

"It's certain," replied Andy, "You're going to be a huge, humongous, egotistical star just like me. Cab drivers will kneel at the sight of your luggage."

"You'll get it; you're going to have little people to thank," I said.

Betty laughed.

"I don't know if you're encouraging or discouraging me," she said.

"I don't think we know either," I said.

"Seriously, Betty, I think it's great. Good job."

"Thank you, Andy."

Betty got up and threw her arms around Andy's shoulders and kissed him on the cheek then bit his ear.

"You were good to me. Thanks," she said. "I wish I could take you with me. Both of you."

Andy smiled, looking up sideways, and patted her wrist.

"We could be your chef and card reader," said Andy, "Your entourage."

"Oh no, you're supposed to be an actor, too," said Betty. She sand¬papered Andy's head with her hand playfully. "And you..."

Betty looked at me.

"I'm a card reader," I said.

"You're not going?" asked Andy, "It's just for a few days."

Betty held still, watching me closely.

"The thing about your art, you have to be able to practice it alone," I said.

Betty shook her head. She leveled an accusing finger at me.

"Except if you want to be a cheerleader," said Betty.

"Or be an elevator operator," said Andy.

"Or be a dental surgeon or manicurist," insisted Betty.

"Or a headhunter or cannibal," challenged Andy.

"A cannibal?" I said.

"Sure, they never eat alone. There's always have another person there."

"Sounds like I'm wrong," I laughed.

"You are and you don't know it," said Betty. She sat back in her chair a moment her hands in her lap, her gaze heavy upon me. Then she laughed and shook her head. It was pity.

"What time do you leave tomorrow?" asked Andy.

"Around nine, the plane takes off at 11:15, in New York by evening."

"Do you want me to come?"

"No, Jean is picking me up and dropping me off at the airport."

"Fabalus," said Andy with New York accent.

Betty said she wanted to dance. She got up and turned up the music. She tugged Andy to his feet and the two bopped and jitterbugged. Andy did the swim, Betty the monkey. Both were laughing at each other.

I sat at the table with my half-eaten crepe. My ankle felt pinched by the knife in my boot.

"We certainly can entertain ourselves," I called.

Betty and Andy descended on me, pulling me up by the underarms onto the dance floor.

"Let's dirty dog," shouted Andy.

We got down and did push-ups to the music until we were flat on our bellies, breathless, laughing like complete fools.

CHAPTER 162

We were sitting on the floor, Betty leaning her back against me. Andy was against his couch, looking at his ceiling, his hands on his chest.

"Let's hear one of your poems, Andy," said Betty. "Andy writes poetry, it's really good."

"Betty," said Andy.

"No, let's hear one, come on, you're not exactly stage shy," said Betty.

"Stage shy? Not the Andy Man," he said.

"So go ahead," coaxed Betty. "Jean would love to hear it, right?"

"Not really," I said. Betty elbowed me.

Andy stood and put his arms out as if expecting the moon to land in them.

"Why I act, by Andrew McKenna," he began.

"I was alone on stage. And it was a circus scene. I had to let in the little and the large. Those with tickets, those without. The naked and the furred. Clowns wearing trash, women trying to wear nothing, the preachers with their boa-constricting collars, life's victims wearing just their faces. The rich with their waddling penguin pride, the poor with their hangdog slobbering. The tightrope walkers of despair with their wildly tipping umbrellas. Children trudging in the ring-around-the-rosie of hope. And worse, I had to let in myself in the middle of all of this. And with the whole circus watching, expecting, hoping, for a leap of mastery, slip from the wire, a funny shovel in the pants, I had to do something, I had to act."

Betty clapped like an alarm clock going off.

"Yay!"

Andy bowed his head nearly to his knees.

"Now you," said Betty. She nudged me with her back.

"I don't know any poetry," I said.

"Tell us about a card. What is the best card?" insisted Betty.

"The best card is the last one. The Universe."

"Why?"

I took a breath.

"Well, it shows a world of balance and completeness. A world of great potential, of capabilities waiting to be seen. You see Beauty rising through the heart of it. The Universe is a card of integration, and the spirit rising toward joy."

"Nice," said Betty.

"And the secret of this card is: it is inside you."

Betty and Andy sat silent a moment.

"Do you believe that?" asked Betty.

"I believe it about you," I said.

"Then why don't you like other people? Why are you holding back?" She gave her head a shake of anger. Her voice was cloudy.

"Other people? You mean the Clayton's and all those other actors of this world? Go to a mall and look at them walking around. All shapes, all sizes. They're just a bunch of monkeys who have lost their tree."

"Ohh!" said Betty as if struck. She blinked her eyes as they teared up.

"I have to go. Thank you, Andy. It was a wonderful party. I have to go." Betty got up without looking at us.

She quickly went to the door and crossed the hall.

We both heard her door lock.

CHAPTER 163

Andy was having trouble finding a place to rest his eyes in his own apartment.

"You better do something, man," he said.

CHAPTER 164

That night I went deep into the park and sat alone.

I wondered if the world made any sense, if there was any meaning to this story. I once had a heretic tell me that God stopped communicating with us because we always asked questions. He got tired. It was like shouting down a well.

I asked about our yearning for eternal truth. He counseled me to become a priest and convert that to yearning for women.

An atheist once told me that there were many many gods, but nobody wanted the job.

To be or not to be was followed by to C or not to C, followed by to D or not to D.

That the number of home runs hit out of Yankee Stadium by monkeys was potentially infinite, but it would be a lousy game.

I sat in the park in a quandary of mind, and spirit, and emotion, and need. It was a night of a million stars. I thought hard.

Somewhere a goldfish stared at the moon.

CHAPTER 165

I went home. I fumbled with my own keys and went into my clean apartment. I was greeted by the slight smell of rotting flowers. I went from room to room till I found the culprit vase and emptied it.

I felt a vague dissatisfaction with all I touched.

I looked about the room feeling contained.

I sniffed at myself, the grand card reader uncertain of what was next.

I felt caught like a stranger in a story.

I didn't want to go to bed though it was late.

I sat down and threw an idle card.

The Emperor. Sometimes known as the Window.

I remembered the meaning of this card.

It means we have to accept our vision, our joys, our rage and pain as our own creations, that what we let into our world is let in by us.

The Emperor means we are our own punishment, we are our own jailers.

And you have to let the prisoners go free.

CHAPTER 166

That morning I knocked on Betty's door. I heard rattling and motion on the other side.

"Who is it?" called Betty.

"It's me," I said.

"Just a minute," she called.

After a bit more rattling, the door opened. Betty's suitcase was sitting there.

Betty looked out at me holding my own suitcase in my hand.

Her face crinkled up and she blinked tears. Her lower lip trembled.

"Oh, you're coming," she said.

She came forward and threw her arms around my neck.

She kissed me.

"Oh why? Why are you coming?" she asked.

"I don't know why," I said.

Trying to smile through her tears, she said, "Maybe we can just take care of each other?"

"For as long as you need me," I said. She kissed me hard.

Betty locked her door.

We picked up our suitcases. We walked down to the street curb and caught a Chariot cab for the airport.

CHAPTER 167

I throw this last card for you:

The Fool.

He goes with an open heart. A firm step. A joyous vision. A happy laugh.

I see a good journey ahead.

www.ingramcontent.com/pod-product-compliance
Lightning Source LLC
Chambersburg PA
CBHW051129020726
47501CB00005B/1418